WH
IF NOT

Jacqueline J. Shulman

When, if not now?

First published by Amazon 2021

ISBN: 9798758946855
Imprint: Independently published

It is the intention of the author to donate profits to ESRA from the Amazon sales of this book. ESRA, Israel's largest English speaking network, is a non-profit organisation run and managed mainly by volunteers. Aside from its wide range of social and cultural activities in English, ESRA runs education and welfare projects aimed at narrowing the socio-economic gaps in Israeli society. Through ESRA's diverse projects, bearing the Midot certification of effectiveness, the lives of countless Israelis have been impacted and improved, and whole communities transformed.

Email: jacquelinejshulman@gmail.com

Cover design: Liora Bloom

WHEN,
IF NOT NOW?

About the author

Jacqueline J. Shulman, known as Jackie, was born in Sunderland, U.K. Since coming to live in Israel in 1979 her career has been diverse, including community worker, medical secretary and antique dealer. Gainfully employed throughout the years, her work has ironically always involved antiquities, whether they were dusty inanimate objects or of the human kind. She is an avid collector of excess clutter including mementos from all corners of the world. In particular hundreds of condiment sets, many received as treasured gifts, which are gradually encroaching on every available space in their home. Although a keen reader, the thought of penning a novel could not have been further from her horizons. Now however, in her early seventies, she has discovered that writing is not only a refreshing pastime, but also a wonderful diversion. She hopes that readers will enjoy this eventful journey as much as she relished writing it. She highly recommends this form of relaxation to anyone looking for a distraction from life's vicissitudes.

Jackie's husband, David, having retired from the legal profession, devotes much of his time to his historical and genealogical website. They have three children and ten grandchildren and live in Raanana, Israel.

Acknowledgements

My thanks go to David, my wonderful, remarkable husband of over fifty years for all his factual advice. Who needs Google when married to David! My son Asa gave me his astute and invaluable input, regarding aspects of the story which he felt were inconsistent.

To Lyn Fisher, a dear and treasured friend who morphed into editor extraordinaire, imparting gems of inestimable value. She lifted my words with her honest critique, skilled analysis and pertinent suggestions. Our literary camaraderie took us on some thrilling journeys. Some I had imagined, but others stirred unique memories of joint holidays, shared in those carefree pre-Corona days. With a myriad of high tech tools at our disposal, we spent many hours in discussion on WhatsApp, whilst at the same time sitting opposite our laptops, sharing our screens for a joint edit.

Using so much technology, I couldn't help but wonder at the masterpieces created by the many famous wordsmiths in bygone days. How did they produce such exquisite penmanship with the aid of nothing more than quill and ink to write their manuscripts? Not even auto-correct!

To my children and grandchildren
The essence of my universe

Author's Note

This is a work of fiction. The main protagonists, Josh and Alistair as well as all the other characters, are total figments of my imagination and the events ascribed to them in this story have no basis in fact. I would add however, that in some instances I have borrowed a trait, hobby or admirable quality from someone whom I have encountered over the years, in order to construct an entirely fabricated scenario. In other cases, an idea may have been sparked by a real event that occurred, whether heroic or horrific. A few well-known personalities do make their appearance, but all incidents and dialogue with them are entirely fictitious.

Prologue

Prayer is one of the most powerful and positive ways of communicating with a deity and in Judaism the core of spiritual life. So why was it that Josh could not concentrate on the prayers he had been saying on and off for almost seventy years. Visions kept creeping into his head, memories which he desperately tried to consign to oblivion. Images of someone who had disappeared abruptly from his life ten years earlier kept parading before him.

In the interim, he had attempted to block her from his thoughts, yet recently she was appearing there more and more persistently. It wasn't only at times when his mind should have been on his prayers. He could be sitting with any one of his nineteen grandchildren, when their face would be transposed into hers. Yang was the only woman he had ever really loved and he had spent five years leading a risky and precarious double life in order to relish and savour that love.

In the North London suburb of Hendon, where he lived with Miriam, his wife of over fifty years, he outwardly embraced the doctrines of the religion, immersing himself in the strictly Orthodox world in which he was highly revered. No one seeing this virtuous man could possibly imagine him leading any other sort of existence.

Yet he had.

Treading a dangerous line between two realms which were planets apart, he had maintained a facade. Once he had stepped onto a path totally alien from the one he normally tread, he knew that he was playing with a fire which could jeopardize the very fabric of his family life. Yet Yang had been like a drug which he could not give up. She had held him captive in her palm for the five years they had been together, and even though ten years had since elapsed, he was still a prisoner to her spell.

Chapter One

"Everything has beauty, but not everyone sees it."
Confucius

Sunday 27th October 2019. Shanghai

China is the most populous country with almost one and a half billion citizens. Josh Green was mulling over this statistic as he sat in a taxi on his way to the Waldorf Astoria Hotel in Shanghai, questioning his rash decision to come. How could he possibly hope to uncover the mystery of Yang's sudden disappearance, when the last time he saw her was ten years ago? There had been no communication since then and he had few clues to establish her present whereabouts, in this immense ocean of mankind.

Their years together had indeed been magical, but Josh had a wife and five children living in a parallel universe and he had always known that his life of duplicity would eventually have to end. As much as he loved Yang, his children were paramount to his very being. Just the thought of divorcing Miriam was abhorrent to him, because of the pain it would inflict on their children, despite the fact they were now all grown up.

Over the years, suitable brides and grooms had been secured for each one. Even if they didn't quite fulfil all Miriam's expectations to begin with, they were nurtured and finely honed by her careful instruction until they did. They had all moved on with families of their own, but none lived far away and all were an inherent component of his life. When he sat in his immaculate study in their beautiful home contemplating his life, as he often did, he knew he had so much to be thankful for. So why, he asked himself, even after ten years, did he still feel the gaping hole, the longing that just went on and on? He was like a castaway marooned on a desert island, having allowed all salvation to pass him by.

They had just celebrated the end of Sukkot, the Feast of Tabernacles and in an impetuous moment, so inconsistent with his normal prudence he had booked a flight to Shanghai. He told Miriam that he had urgent business in China and was not sure how long it would take. Her concern with his business affairs had long since waned, along with her interest in him. Although he had officially retired from his law office, he still kept his hand in as a consultant. He was a valuable asset to them, as he was able to fly off at a moment's notice, when his expertise was required. Miriam would have no reason to question this trip.

Now that he was actually here in China, it was he who was questioning the reason and sanity of his decision, which was nothing more than a capricious and fanciful whim. Could he hope to obliterate the memories, by trying to uncover the enigma of her disappearance? Just like the gratification he felt on completion of a legal matter, perhaps closure would enable him to put her memory behind him.

His reflections continued as he entered the foyer of the hotel. He chose it after recalling a colleague describing it as one of the most impressive hotels he had ever visited. Indeed, with its white marble columns and crystal chandeliers adorning the lobby, it permeated an aura of glamour and opulence. The rest of the hotel melded the historic parts with the new modern tower, a clever hybrid giving the whole edifice a majestic splendour.

Once settled in his bedroom, Josh was sorely tempted to stay there. It was no less luxurious than the rest of the hotel and room service was readily available. As he perused the list of amenities, he indulged himself in the fantasy of a week of total decadence in his room. A whole host of services were offered including massages, pedicures and manicures. A coffee machine and a well-stocked mini bar were on hand and at a cost, he could even have his own personal butler to pamper him. He could soak in the deep inviting bathtub, using the expensive creams and lotions arranged carefully around the bathroom, while watching television at the same time.

Reality jolted him out of his lethargy. It had been a long, tiring flight and his watch still showed ten o'clock in the morning, but local time was six o'clock in the evening. In order to acclimatise, he knew he must be practical and as much as he was inclined to give in to the temptations of sleep, he needed to keep going for another two or three hours. Reluctantly, he dragged himself off the bed and had a shower, knowing that if he stepped into the bathtub, he would be asleep within seconds. He dressed himself in order to go down to the hotel's famed long bar, which stretched for 110 feet and was supposedly one of the longest bars ever constructed.

On leaving his room he almost collided with the young man who was just leaving the adjoining one. 'Sorry' he muttered, reprimanding himself. Joshy boy, you must concentrate on the present, instead of allowing your mind to wander all the time. He loved to call himself Joshy boy; it had been Yang's term of endearment for him. Whilst they waited for the elevator, he tried to engage the young man in conversation, asking him if he was on holiday, but he turned his back on Josh. Presumably he had not forgiven him.

The iconic long bar was indeed aptly named. He glanced at the book sitting on the lustrous dark mahogany counter with the title "*The Waldorf Astoria Bar Book*." After much deliberation he consulted with the highly professional bartender, whose tag labelled him as a mixologist named Don. Eventually he settled on the spiced tangerine apple whiskey cocktail, grateful for Don's advice. How could he have chosen from the infinite list of exotic sounding drinks such as the cooling '*Blue Lagoon,*' the seductive '*Between the Sheets*' and the always popular '*Peacock Alley.*'

Taking his drink over to one of the comfortable armchairs, he sat down to relax and take in the scene. There was an atmosphere of vitality, yet he found himself sinking dreamily into his thoughts. His mind wandered back to a vision of Yang smiling up at him alluringly. The problem was, with memory came desire and that was the one thing he was trying desperately to exorcise.

He knew he was considered a bastion of his community, knowledgeable, well liked and especially loved by all the children who called him Mr. Sweetie. After prayers each week, he would distribute sweets to the children from the large bag he kept in his locker.

His community had been sympathetic to his plight when, for five long years, he had to travel to Israel weekly for work. 'Poor man,' they might have been heard muttering aloud to themselves. 'Having to leave his delightful family during the week, only coming back for the weekend. What a lonely miserable life.' They would never risk the transgression of gossiping. "*Thou shalt not go up and down as a talebearer among the people.*"

Oh how far from the truth!

What would they think had they known that his days in Israel had been one long sunset of sheer joy and love? Had the truth been uncovered, the scandal would have rocked the community and been ruinous for his inconsolable family. It would be asked how a man, who often led the community in prayers with his sweet soulful voice, could commit such a despicable act.

So deeply engrossed in his musings, he didn't notice the man who sat down at the table next to him, clutching a large flat box to his chest, muttering to himself. Emerging from his reverie, Josh was distressed to discern the words 'such heartbreak, such a loss.'

Josh hoped for the sake of this stranger, that the order of bereavement had not been turned on its head.

'A parent?' he asked delicately.

'No' he whispered, 'a snuff bottle.' Amidst all his laments and sighs Josh presumed that he had misheard the stranger, but when the man continued 'the most cherished and priceless snuff bottle of my collection, GONE,' Josh realised that he had in fact heard correctly.

Recovering his equilibrium, the stranger apologised for his emotional and self-indulgent outburst. 'Please allow me to introduce myself. I am Alastair Sylvester. I am a collector of rare Chinese inside-painted snuff bottles and one of my most prized possessions has mysteriously disappeared from my collection.'

At this point Alistair opened the box he was cradling to his chest and removed a large book which was carefully wrapped in tissue paper. He moved over to show Josh the book, opening it at a picture of the object in question. The snuff bottle was certainly a work of art, as was the book itself. A thick hardback with pages and pages of glossy photos, depicting examples of snuff bottles all delicately painted from the inside, as well as featuring Chinese art in its many forms. The front cover was thicker than the back one, with a cavity in the centre in which an actual glass snuff bottle was displayed, secured by a thin piece of perspex.

'This is a catalogue of my collection and I have come to China in the hope of tracking down my missing treasure, since the perpetrators of the theft could be Chinese. I speak Mandarin so I don't have problems navigating my way round the more disreputable dealers. Forgive me though I've been very rude, speaking about my problems when I see you are visibly immersed in deep thoughts of your own.'

Introducing himself, Josh explained that he had just arrived from London and was feeling quite weary.

'Ah London,' the stranger repeated, 'the country's in a bit of a turmoil at present with the whole Brexit mess, to say nothing of Corbyn and all the problems the poor Queen has with her family. I am glad that I no longer live there.'

'Please, please' Josh said as he gestured with his hand, 'I've come here to get away from all that.'

'Sorry' Alistair apologized with a sympathetic smile. 'I left the UK some years ago and relocated to Rome, so I take great pleasure in riling my British friends.' Josh found himself warming to this man who appeared to be relishing their banter. When he spoke, Alastair Sylvester's face was animated and there was something comical in his expressions. His appearance reflected an intriguing paradox. He exuded an air of elegance and prosperity, with his tailored jacket complete with paisley kerchief over a polo neck sweater, designer jeans and custom-made shoes. All this was at variance with the Chinese-style plait snaking out from the back of his full head of silver hair impeccably combed back, giving him an endearingly flamboyant appearance. Alastair reminded Josh of a theatrical character, although he couldn't remember which one.

It occurred to Josh that since it was highly unlikely he would ever meet this stranger again, and since he spoke Mandarin, perhaps he might be able to give Josh advice on where to start on his own search. Accordingly he confided the true reason for his presence in China.

'Perhaps I can help you.' Alistair suggested. 'I am quite knowledgeable about the intricacies of China; I speak the language and over the years have shown many friends around Shanghai. Tang, my regular driver is readily available and I would happily be your guide. I love the mixture of romance and mystique so we could work as a team, each of us pursuing the mystery of our own missing treasure.' Heartened by the prospect of such a competent ally to assist him, hope welled up in Josh's heart, as he eagerly agreed to Alistair's proposition. Alistair seemed genuinely glad but then added:

'There is just one thing I think I should mention - I am gay.'

'Excellent, excellent, I am Jewish so we both belong to a mistreated minority.'

Chapter Two

"The question isn't who is going to let me;
it's who is going to stop me."
Ayn Rand

Monday 28th October 2019. Shanghai

Meeting together for breakfast, Alistair asked Josh if he knew anything at all about Yang's family. 'Surprisingly enough, I knew her parents quite well.' His mind flitted back almost fifteen years to the time when Yang had first moved in with him. Her parents had come to Israel for a week's visit from China and stayed for three months. They didn't seem to mind the inconvenience of sleeping in the lounge of their small apartment in Rishon Lezion, a town just to the south of Tel Aviv.

'So let's start with the names of her parents' Alistair suggested, 'although the problem is that Chinese names are different from Western ones. The family name comes first and most of those have only one syllable, encompassing about eighty five percent of China's citizens. One advantage for our search, traditionally a married woman doesn't take on her husband's family name, but keeps her own unchanged. If she is in China and has married in the meantime, that would not be an obstacle.' The very thought of Yang marrying someone else provoked irrational and insane feelings of jealousy inside Josh's head.

'I do have their names and an address where I know they were living in Shanghai up to ten years ago.' Again, Josh's mind went back to their strange visit. Yang's mother Liat, who was actually a number of years younger than Josh himself, didn't seem to be at all perturbed by her daughter's suitor being a married man almost thirty years Yang's senior. Over the years he had wondered if she really was a sweet little Chinese mother, with only her daughter's best interest at heart, or was she involved in something more sinister. She had, after all, presented Josh with an extremely expensive sapphire ring, which she suggested he use to propose to Yang. At the time he hadn't questioned its origins. In fact there had been occasions when he suspected Liat was giving him vibes not purely of an affectionate motherly nature, or was it just his overactive imagination? At forty-five, Liat was a very attractive lady and she could quite easily have been mistaken for Yang's sister, not her mother.

'What is their address?' Alistair asked, raising an eyebrow at the response. 'Quite an upscale area' he pointed out. 'Let's check it out this evening. I have a busy day today meeting fine art dealers and old colleagues, so I suggest we meet at eight in the lobby.'

Was he on a route to disaster? Josh couldn't help but ask himself, as they were driven through a residential area of Shanghai. Would he regret this impulsive decision to open Pandora's Box? Perhaps, if it wasn't for Alistair spurring him forward, he would have abandoned this whole mad escapade and just basked in the luxury of his bedroom for a week. After all, Yang had left in haste, telling him not to come after her. He recalled the shock when he returned to an empty apartment in Israel, after being in London for his usual weekend at home. She had left him a letter which he had read and re-folded so many times that the words had become indistinct, but each one had been etched on his heart.

November 2009

> *"Dearest Josh, thank you for five incredible years. I am sorry that I have to leave you like this but I must return to China. I will not be coming back and I beg you, never try to find me. You can love someone immeasurably but still choose to say goodbye. I will always love you and will constantly cherish our glorious times together, but I choose to say goodbye. Together or apart I will always be your adoring precious amethyst."*

There had also been a letter of resignation at work, apologising to her colleagues for leaving, stating personal reasons for her immediate return to China. Stunned and desolate, the thought of suspicious circumstances had not entered Josh's head at that time. Even if they had, how could he have possibly shared his fears with anyone?

It was only when he had been back in Hendon for a number of months that he found her necklace amongst his belongings and doubts began to creep into his mind. Josh knew how thrilled she had been when he bought it for her birthday. Made from colourful semi-precious stones, she had been fascinated to learn that in the Hebrew Bible a different gemstone represents each of the twelve tribes. Expecting her to wear it round her neck, he had been bemused when she put it round her slim waist accentuating the contours of her body, assuring him that she would treasure it forever and *never* take it off. She pointed out that in certain cultures, waist adornments were associated with sensuality and fertility.

With the discovery of the necklace, further disturbing thoughts began to plague his mind. Why had she addressed him as Josh instead of Joshy Boy, in the note she left? Why had she signed the letter "your adoring precious amethyst?" When he gave her the necklace and went through the names of all the stones, he told her she was his precious jewel.

'Can't I be your precious amethyst' she had entreated, as she informed him that the ancient Chinese believed that the amethyst stone prevented nightmares.

'No' he had replied, 'I am your Joshy Boy and you are my precious jewel.' Could the reference to the amethyst be a camouflaged indication of some sort of nightmare?

As they arrived in the leafy suburb where grand colonial style houses nestled in verdant gardens, Josh was becoming more and more nervous, knowing that this search for Yang's parents could unleash a difficult or even dangerous situation. Too late for misgivings, Alistair had emerged from the car and was already ringing the bell outside the ornate wrought iron gates.

They were flooded in light as a male voice came over the intercom in an aggressive tone. Unfazed, Alistair replied, in what to Josh sounded like fluent Chinese and gave the name of the family they were looking for. After a short response in an unmistakably hostile tone, the intercom clicked and the light was extinguished, cloaking the area in darkness. Climbing back into the car Josh looked at Alistair with a questioning expression.

'I gave him the name of Yang's parents and using the choicest Chinese words, he told me that we must have made a mistake. He has occupied the house for the last twenty years.'

'How very strange' Josh murmured, 'I know that I used to post letters from Yang to her parents at this address.' He wasn't sure if he was disappointed or relieved. He had tried and failed, so perhaps he should now abandon the whole insane idea. Alistair, on the other hand, was even more eager to resolve the intrigue.

On the drive back, Alistair speculated over possible scenarios and explanations for this puzzling outcome. Pulling up to the hotel, Tang, their driver said to Alistair 'I don't want to worry you, but a car has been tailing us all the way since you visited that house. Probably just coincidence,' he added, 'as it drove on when we pulled up here, but I thought I should mention it.' Alistair translated the conversation for Josh's benefit before they parted company, agreeing to meet at breakfast to rethink their strategy.

Drifting in and out of sleep, Josh became weightless, as he floated into a cold menacing no-man's land, waking up with relief when he became aware that the person attacking him was only in his nightmare. Now sleep was evading him and his mind was becoming more lucid, with a jumble of frightening thoughts rushing through his head.

Had his brain been so besotted by her beauty, her love and yes her lust for him, that he had been blinded and ignored any danger signals? At the time, he hadn't even given it a thought when Yang's mother had brought her a fake driving license and two fake passports, one with her name slightly altered. He knew that her mother had paid a Tel Aviv low-life to travel to Cyprus with Yang, so they could marry, to ensure that she could stay in Israel. It was simply a marriage of convenience Yang had stressed to Josh, when she had moved in with him and had assured him that, at great cost, the scoundrel had agreed to a divorce. Where had that money come from Josh now questioned? He had been adamant that he would not live with her if she was married. Although he knew it was hypocritical, the last thing he wanted was to be involved with someone else's wife.

His mind went back to the time they first met in 2004. The Intifada in Israel was weakening and foreigners were again considering investments there. As a partner in a successful London law firm, Josh had been delighted when his senior partners had suggested that he join their recently established overseas office in Tel Aviv. Their wealthiest, most influential client wanted to invest staggering sums in Israeli institutions and businesses. Josh was considered the ideal person to deal with this, since he spoke Hebrew and even had Israeli citizenship. It was agreed that he would be flown back to London every Thursday night or Friday morning so that he could be with his family.

Ever since Josh had received the book "*Exodus*" by Leon Uris at the age of thirteen for a bar-mitzvah gift, he had harboured a yearning to live in Israel.

He had beseeched his parents to let him go to Israel when he finished school but they insisted that he attend university first in the UK. A compromise had been reached. His parents suggested that he spend a year at a yeshiva, a Jewish theological college in Israel, on the understanding that he would return and take up his place at LSE to study law. The University had been willing to defer his place for a year.

Josh loved living in Israel and his fluency in Hebrew improved by the day. Studying the sacred texts and discussing the minutiae of all the religious laws each day and sometimes long into the night, was very often too intense for him. On these occasions, it wasn't unusual to find him devouring a burger in downtown Jerusalem, or even busking with his guitar on the famous King George

Street, singing hits by the Beatles and his particular favourite, Bob Marley.

At the time his resolve to return to Israel had been absolute and, unbeknown to his parents, he had even taken out Israeli citizenship, but as soon as he was back in London, daily life had intervened. Once qualified, he knew that it would be foolhardy to go to Israel as a penniless graduate, so he had joined an eminent law firm, intending to accumulate enough money and experience before emigrating. Fate had a different agenda for him. He was offered a partnership, married and had children before reaching the age of fifty-five without achieving his dream. He knew that his partner's suggestion would now be the only opportunity to fulfil that ambition, albeit partially.

Busy acclimatising to the new Israeli office, he was barely aware of the young Chinese girl who worked as one of the trainee lawyers, helping him with his research. All he knew was that she was very determined to qualify as a lawyer and spent hours helping him search for any documentation he needed.

So how did it happen that a man of his standing embarked on a relationship so alien to the high standards he always set for himself? Although he did not adhere strictly to all the precepts of Judaism, he had a deep abiding love for his religion, which was essential to his very being.

He had been so preoccupied at work one day, he was astonished when he glanced at his watch, and discovered it was already nine thirty. Leaving the office, he walked past the central area, where to his consternation he found Yang asleep in her chair. He tried to wake her, but she seemed to be in a deep sleep, despite her unnatural position. His concern deepened when he saw a box of painkillers on her desk and he began to imagine the worst case scenario, until to his relief, he saw that there was only one missing from the packet. Knowing he couldn't leave her there, Josh also knew that it would be considered inappropriate for a religious man to pick her up and move her somewhere more comfortable.

He went in search of some assistance, but to his dismay, he discovered they were the only two left in the office. Now Josh was in a quandary. As well as the religious aspect, the issue of sexual harassment was definitely of concern. The subject had generated much debate when everyone in the office had received an internal memo, stating that the Managing Partner of the office would be monitoring all complaints of this nature. Although the subject provoked mirth around the office, Josh knew it needed to be taken seriously. He had been speaking to a lawyer from another company who told Josh that he had been called into a disciplinary hearing, accused of sexual harassment. Having no idea what he had done, he thought it must be a mistake, but it turned out that his misdemeanour occurred when he had walked into the kitchen, where a young female colleague was crying. In what he thought was a perfectly natural gesture he had put an arm around her, simply in an expression of comfort as he might do with his daughter. It appeared that his kindness had been misconstrued.

As Josh stood there debating his options, Yang gave a sudden shudder and he feared that she could fall out of the chair, injuring herself. Again he tried to wake her but she was too deeply asleep, so despite his initial concerns, he decided to move her. Gently, he gathered her in his arms in order to carry her to the one comfortable couch in the whole office. Looking down at her delicately sculpted face, Josh was shocked by two things that happened simultaneously. Her arms tightened around his shoulders and she murmured in her sleep. 'Oh Josh, I love you so much' and he felt a stirring in his loins.

Extricating himself from her grasp and putting her down on the couch, a piece of paper she was clutching fluttered to the floor. When he picked it up, he couldn't help but notice his name written in elaborate lettering at the top. Presuming it was work related he read it, but was totally unprepared for what he saw.

"*You show me kindness in little ways,*
Bringing sunshine to my darkest days.
Though you barely know that I exist,
In my dreams, it is by you I'm kissed.

My love for you grows more each day,
But to you, of course I would never say.
So I simply love you from afar,

Josh, my brilliant guiding star.

And I would give to you the sky above,
For the smallest shred of your love.
I am enraptured by your charms,
Oh just once, to be held in your arms.

At that moment Yang opened her eyes, which grew wide in ecstatic wonderment, turning quickly into horrified embarrassment as the realization of the situation hit her. She floundered, trying to apologize, but Josh put his fingers to her lips, evoking an electrifying touch, a cosmic spark which changed everything.

Affairs of the heart are tricky things. By the time he realised what he was doing, that trivial gesture, a foolishness which could have been instantly extinguished turned into a pivotal life-changing moment. Why had he not merely dismissed the incident? Was it the allure of the unknown or was it vanity?

Growing up, Josh had been an awkward gangling youth, spotty and bespectacled. When he matured he had never quite thrown off such a self-image, having no idea that the chrysalis had burst its shell and transformed into a tall slim handsome man. Totally unwittingly, he had set the female staff abuzz when he first arrived in the Tel Aviv office, and they had likened him to a popular Israeli film star.

Whatever the initial reason for allowing himself to pursue such an unwise course, from that moment onwards, their relationship had developed steadily. Perhaps it was recognition of the primal element of love, for him an elusive quality in his life. Whatever it was, he often pinched himself to acknowledge that this sweet human being actually idolised him and he was hopelessly in love with her. Yang had expressed disbelief when he revealed his age of fifty-five, but this did not diminish her devotion for him and he in turn loved everything about her, especially her youth, vibrancy and innocence.

Once he was sure that Yang wanted to stay with him, he had moved out of his Tel Aviv apartment and moved to an older area of Rishon Lezion where they could blend in unnoticed. So began the sublime bliss which lasted for five truly wondrous years.

Serious and intent, at the same time Yang energized him with her vivacity. She encouraged him to be frivolous and *chill out,* an expression she frequently used, in their moments of relaxation together. Loving music, Yang was delighted when he returned early one Monday morning from his usual trip, with a guitar strung over his shoulder. She even persuaded him to buy coloured shirts instead of the plain white ones he always wore, and he took pride in matching them up with a kipa, the traditional head covering, of the same colour.

Josh embarked on a new unrecognizable version of himself. Back in Hendon at weekends, he reverted to his religious persona, immersing himself in his strictly-orthodox, or as it was known, Haredi existence. A world which encompassed a strict interpretation and adherence to the code of Jewish law and a rejection of modern secular culture. Did he like this new image? Was it completely out of character? He hated to admit it to himself but perhaps since their marriage, cracks had always been lurking within the confines of his nature, although never allowed to break through. Josh had tried to embrace his strictly Orthodox journey for Miriam's sake and subsequently, for their children. However once he infiltrated a domain so diametrically opposed to the one he normally inhabited, he knew he was taking a chance which could ruin the very essence of his family. Yet Yang was an addiction which he simply could not give up. He knew the dangers, but he had traversed his Rubicon. By crossing that fateful line there was no retreat.

In Israel, he took every possible precaution to perpetuate the illusion of religious piety lest word should filter back. Although he didn't wear the black garb or sport a beard generally associated with the Haredi community, he always kept his head covered. An exposed head was a very revealing sign that someone had forsaken the tenets of their religion.

They were seldom seen out together, but on rare occasions, Josh took pity on Yang and decided to take a calculated risk. She never complained, but he knew that occasionally she felt rejected when, out of necessity, she was excluded from his pursuits. On her birthday, Yang begged him to take her to a concert and against his better judgement he acquiesced. When the theatre lights dimmed and it looked like he had not been spotted, his relief was palpable. The next day however, he received a phone call from a close family friend from England on holiday in Israel. He could not disguise the disapproval in his voice when he told Josh that he had seen him at the concert together with a stunning young Chinese girl. Josh weighed up his options. To entrust the friend with his secret, or to concoct the story that two tickets had been on offer from work and he had taken one, with no idea who had taken the second one. He decided not to burden his friend with a truth which could put him in an awkward situation, so he gave the alternative account, which he hoped sounded plausible.

Another time they had walked round to their local parade of shops together. Since they lived in an older part of Rishon Lezion, he thought it was highly unlikely that they would bump into anyone he knew. It was a slightly rundown area with many old dwellings, home to an aging community of immigrants, who had arrived in the years after the State, was declared in 1948. Interspersed were new apartments, which had sprouted up when the old resident of a house had passed away and the land was sold for redevelopment. Josh had chosen a first-floor flat in a block which, despite its age, had a certain character to it.

Approaching the shops, Yang suggested they look for some new cutlery in the hardware store, where the owner was always sitting outside, on display along with his wares. Josh wondered if he sat at the front simply because there was no space for a chair inside. Like an Aladdin's cave, it was a maze of aisles. Goods were piled high, many of them probably even more antiquated than the owner. Wandering up and down with childlike delight, Yang spotted a condiment set in the form of a cottage. 'Let's buy it,' she suggested eagerly. With an enduring smile Josh launched into a lengthy rationale of all the reasons not to buy it.

'First of all, the flat is too small to house the many little ornaments you buy each time you see something cute or quaint. Secondly, it's not quite in accordance with the Feng Shui philosophy you told me about and,' he pointed out 'we have a perfectly good condiment set at home.'

With this final summation he was quite horrified when he heard a voice from the other side of the aisle say

'Go on Josh, buy your wife the condiment set.' He froze in stunned silence as he tried to place the voice. As it dawned on him, he hissed to Yang to leave the shop immediately and go back home. At the same time, he went in the opposite direction, checking as he did that he had not forgotten his head covering. Manoeuvring himself round the corner, with contrived delight and amazement he greeted his old Rabbi.

'Rabbi Singer, what a pleasure. Whatever are you doing here?'

'Since my dear Lottie passed away I've been very lonely in London with all my children now in Israel. I am living in Jerusalem near one of my sons, but my daughter has recently moved to Rishon. Although she lives on the other side of town, this shop is renowned for its good quality merchandise at reasonable prices, so I decided to come and look.' Throughout their conversation he kept looking over Josh's shoulder, querying where his wife had disappeared to. Josh apologized but told him with an uncomfortable laugh, that she had a sudden call of nature and had to rush off.

When he returned to the flat, they had joked about it and he had tried to see the funny side of the situation, but in his heart he knew that this deceit would inevitably have to end.

Shortly afterwards, Yang had disappeared and he made the decision to leave Tel Aviv. They no longer needed his expertise in the office and he knew it was time to put this chapter of his life behind him. It didn't stop him from re-enacting scenes as if they were old movies and thinking constantly about her luscious body.

Over the years, since his permanent return to the U.K. his sense of foreboding had intensified. Perhaps something untoward had befallen Yang. Could the Tel Aviv low-life who her mother had found, possibly have shadowy Chinese connections. Otherwise how had her mother made contact with him, when she had been in China at the time? Could he somehow have located Yang at their flat in Rishon, compelled her to write the letters to allay suspicion, then forcibly abducted her?

Of course, there could be a less chilling reason for her sudden disappearance. Had she returned to marry the brilliant technology student she had dated before she went to study in England? She had spoken about his genius, certain that he was destined to make a big impact in the field of telecommunications. Apparently he wanted to marry her and had been desolate when she decided to go away and study law at Sheffield University. He became obsessed with the idea of developing the technology which would enable him to actually see her when they spoke. Such technology was now readily available and a company called Zoom was being widely used. He had never used it himself but some of the lawyers at work did, for conference calls with colleagues in other countries, which saved them traveling. Josh had read that the founder was Chinese. Perhaps it was her boyfriend who had developed it.

He should be glad if she had found true happiness. Perhaps he was a multi-millionaire and Yang was living a life of untold luxury. That would be an infinitely preferable outcome to the ominous alternatives he had visualized over the years. His rational mind told him he would be content to know she was safe and happy, but his totally perverse feelings of selfishness told him he would be inconsolable if she had found true love with someone else.

So what, he asked himself, was he actually hoping to find, on this journey of discovery?

Chapter Three

"An Investment in knowledge pays the best interest."
Benjamin Franklin

Tuesday 29th October 2019. Shanghai

When they met the next morning, Alistair exuded unbridled enthusiasm for their search. Josh knew deep inside that this pursuit was total foolishness, an indulgence of pure stupidity. Perhaps he could divert Alistair's focus by inquiring about his own life and his love of snuff bottles. As he expected, Alistair was more than willing to elaborate, with his inimitable loquacious flow.

'I was born in England but we moved to the Sultanate of Brunei when I was two, as my father was involved in the oil industry. My mother was from an influential family and became a lady-in-waiting to the Sultan's wife, so I had quite a privileged upbringing, which might sound exotic. In truth though, our great house was for me, a mausoleum. My mother was a remote aloof figure, not even slightly maternal. Consequently I was an only child, brought up and home-schooled by a succession of governesses, each one increasingly more formidable than the last. That is, until Irene arrived.

Irene came when I was ten. She had grown up in a Welsh mining village where her father, and his father before him, had been coal miners. She used to describe the abysmal conditions her father had to work in all day long, descending the mine shaft of the colliery in a lift, shuffling or crawling along the floor to reach the seam, then using deafening drills to remove the coal in order to load it on a truck. He would return home covered in black soot from head to foot and they would bring out the tin bath, place it in the centre of the living room, where he would scrub all the day's grime from his skin.

Determined that this sort of life would not be her destiny, nor that of her younger brother, Irene would knit feverishly each day, stitch after stitch skilfully executed, producing finely crafted children's garments. She sold them to neighbouring mothers, who otherwise could never have afforded such good quality clothes. Every penny was put aside to enable them both to go on to further education and her pride in their achievements was clear. Extremely bright and well read, Irene even managed to beguile my mother with her natural beauty and melodic Welsh lilt. Unfortunately, when her father succumbed to the lung disease prevalent amongst miners she had to return home. We kept in touch from time to time and I was overjoyed when she wrote and told me that she was engaged to the doctor attending her father.

My interest in snuff bottles began when I was ten. My father often travelled and that year he brought me a gift of a Chinese glass snuff bottle, exquisitely painted with the figure of a Shih Tzu dog. I was totally intrigued by its beauty, and curious about the skill that went into painting it from the inside. I loved it so much that each time my father travelled, he would bring me another one on his return.

I learnt that snuff bottles are a microcosm of the craftsmanship of Chinese artisans, sparking my lifelong fascination with China's history and art.

When Irene left I was twelve, so my parents decided that it would be best for my future if I went to a boarding school in England and I was duly dispatched to Rugby. My mother thought I was far too sensitive. She hoped that being made to play a sport like rugby would make a man of me. I was absolutely petrified, as I had read Tom Brown's schooldays, based on Thomas Hughes days at Rugby School.'

'Was it as bad as you anticipated?'

'No, things had improved since those days and for the first time in my life I had friends. I was quite content to be there, although I did hate playing rugby, which needless to say was an obligatory part of the sports curriculum. Unfairly I ended up with the nickname Cinderella.'

Why?'

'Because I kept running away from the ball,' Alistair replied with a smile. 'Every time I passed the statue of William Webb Ellis I cursed him. Why did he have to pick up the ball and run with it, creating the *"rugby"* style of play?

When I was eighteen, I gained a place in the faculty of East Asian Studies at Cambridge. I joined the famous

Footlights dramatic club, and went on to attain a small amount of success in the entertainment industry. I realised that I was gay during that time, but then it was considered a totally unacceptable way of life, so I had to keep it a secret. Some years later I took up residence in Rome where I befriended a group of Italian opera mavens. I learnt their beautiful language, something of an antidote to Chinese, and decided to make my permanent home in Italy. So there you have it, my potted history!'

'Where do you display all your snuff bottles?' enquired an enthralled Josh.

'Some of them are on show in specially-built cabinets but a lot of them are carefully wrapped and protected in custom-made drawers. Whenever I return from a trip I rotate the bottles and put any new ones in my cabinet.'

'Why don't you display them all?' Josh enquired curiously.

'As with other collections, if too many are exhibited, the senses become confused and the intrinsic value of such beauty is lost. In the meantime, my collection has become renowned through the International Chinese Snuff Bottle Society and recently I was invited to exhibit at a Museum in Washington. In order to prepare for the exhibition I compiled this book as a showcase for every single bottle in my possession. Although numerous editions were published, the copy with an actual snuff bottle inserted into its cover is unique. It encapsulates the three most significant aspects of my life. My father whom I idolized, my dog who I adore and my snuff bottles which are my lifeblood.

The exhibition was a huge success, and I was amazed by the amount of favourable coverage I received from the press. Sadly, in the end this was not to my benefit because when it came to packing up the collection, I discovered that my most coveted and much admired acquisition was missing. As a large number of Chinese had visited the exhibition, it was suggested that perhaps Shanghai was where I should start my search, so here I am. I've been meeting with various dealers to see if any of them might have been offered my bottle, but so far none of them has any recollection of seeing it.

I hope you will forgive me,' Alistair continued, 'but I have also made some discreet enquiries on your behalf. A company called Kung Fu International Investigations, based in Shanghai specialises in locating missing persons. I've taken the liberty of scheduling an appointment for later today.' Seeing the look of eagerness on Alistair's face, Josh did not have the heart to tell him that he no longer wanted to pursue the matter. Hiding his qualms of doubt, he agreed.

At five thirty they were ushered into the Kung Fu Agency by a portly character resembling Humpty Dumpty with a generous pot belly, a moon-shaped face and a little black hat perched comically on top of his head. He fussed about, moving papers and files from the chairs so they could sit down.

'I am Mr. Wong. I can locate lover, debtor, birth parents and much more. We use latest technologies and databases. You will be astounded at results. Please tell me full name, address and any other information you have.' Josh gave him Yang's family name, Gongzi, as well as the names of her parents, Sammy and Liat.

He went on to inform Mr. Wong that the previous evening he and Alistair had visited the address Josh had for her parents, but in no uncertain terms, had been assured that they must have been mistaken. Josh kept to himself any concerns he had about having been followed on their way back, or any of his other suspicions. After all, these could simply be more of his insane delusions.

Josh continued with the scant information he had. 'Yang grew up in China but since her father spent some time working in Belize, he procured a Belizean passport for her. She studied law at Sheffield University in the UK where she befriended an Israeli girl. This friend spoke about Israel with such love and enthusiasm, urging Yang to visit during their summer break. Although reluctant to go at first, once she arrived, she was overwhelmed by the vibrancy of the country and decided to stay. Ten years ago Yang disappeared from my life, leaving a note saying she was returning to China.'

At this point, Josh preferred not to mention that Yang had been adamant that he should not look for her.

'So you want good news first yes? Gongzi is unusual surname. If it was Wang, Li or Zhang, twenty percent of

China shares this name. Bad news for you, the meaning is "*to pay*".' He obviously found it highly amusing as he imparted this information and continued, chuckling as he said 'now let's get down to monkey business. Do you like comedy? In evenings I am stand-up comedian. Perhaps you come and see my show.'

Without taking a breath he then asked 'How do the Chinese name their children? They drop a broom out of the window and see what sound it makes. That is why we have so many called Ching, Chang and Chong.' He was still laughing at his joke as he saw them out, with assurances that he would be in touch soonest.' As they left, Alistair observed wryly, 'I certainly hope that his investigational skills are an improvement on his ability as a comedian.'

Driving along the waterfront towards their hotel, the sun was just beginning to set, giving the skyline along the Bund an ethereal beauty of yellow and orange hues.

'This area is a protected historical district' Alistair noted as he asked Josh 'do you know about the Bund's Jewish connections?'

'I picked up a guide book at the airport which alluded to it, but with little detail. I'll be happy if you fill me in.'

'Actually, the city's long Jewish history has been an integral part of its present day success, due to a number of prominent Sephardic families like the Sassoons, Hardoons and Kadoories. In fact a synagogue built by the Hardoon family near the Bund provided refuge for a Talmudic seminary during the war.'

'Yes of course,' Josh exclaimed. 'It was the Mir Yeshiva. I learnt about that when I studied at a Yeshiva myself, in Jerusalem.'

'Another notable figure, Sir Victor Sassoon built extensively in Shanghai with a number of properties on the Bund. If you look to your right, there is the Peace Hotel also known as Sassoon House. When it was completed in 1929, it was considered the Bund's crown jewel as it was one of the first skyscrapers, but even more important, it had indoor plumbing. Sir Victor was from a Baghdadi family who made their fortune in the opium business. He came here via India and England, where he attended Trinity College, Cambridge, which just happens to be my Alma Mater, and where I first heard his name mentioned.'

'Perhaps Vidal Sassoon was from the same family,' Josh mused, as his mind wandered back to the days leading up to his bar-mitzvah in December 1962. His mother announced that she had made a hair appointment at the famed Vidal Sassoon salon in Bond Street. The family could hardly believe their eyes when she returned. The transformation was dramatic. When she left home in the morning she was wearing her usual dowdy clothing, with her lacquered beehive hairstyle atop her head. She returned in a brand new Mary Quant outfit and a sleek geometrical hairstyle which accentuated the contours of her face. Josh could still remember his father's words when he saw her, *"Well, if I wasn't already in love with you, I would be falling in love all over again."*

In the eyes of thirteen year-old Josh he had always thought of his mother as ancient, but on that day he saw her anew, with the realisation that she wasn't even forty.

'On reflection, I doubt Vidal Sassoon was related. As far as I know, he came from a very poor London family.'

Alistair continued to expound. 'As you can see, the buildings are of various architectural styles from Renaissance and Baroque to Art Deco. Over the years they have housed many important institutions. In its heyday, during the 1920s and 1930s our hotel was the most exclusive men's social club for British nationals in Shanghai. It was taken over by the Waldorf Astoria a few years ago. Perhaps tomorrow we can spend the day sightseeing. I'd like to take you to the marble hall built by Sir Ellie Kadoorie, as well as some stunning gardens and other sights.'

Back in his room, Josh pondered over the fact that he knew so little about Yang's life growing up in China. He knew she was an only child in accordance with government policy. He had heard that restrictions had now eased, but couples still had to apply for permission to have a second child. Josh cast his mind back to the time Yang thought she might be pregnant. She had been elated until she understood how angry Josh had been. He had rushed to the pharmacy to buy a pregnancy test and the magnitude of his relief was equally matched by the magnitude of her disappointment. Of course she must have wanted children, but he had been adamant that this could never happen between them. He had five strictly-orthodox children in London, and was certainly not going to father a non-Jewish Chinese child in Israel. Shortly afterwards, he had taken her to a gynaecologist to be fitted with a contraceptive device, ensuring that there would be no more scares in the future.

When he thought about those euphoric heady days, he compared the enormity of the disparities between the two opposing worlds he had inhabited. In Hendon, a man of his stature would never be seen buying such intimate items as a pregnancy test, tampons or heaven forbid, ladies underwear. Such subjects were completely taboo for men in their circles. Reminiscing over his life, Josh thought about the great gulf that lay between his background, growing up in a modern orthodox society and Miriam's, raised in the strictly-orthodox community of Stamford Hill.

He mulled over their lives together and how they met. Her family were part of the Haredi world, but at eighteen she had been a rebel, almost considered the black sheep of their large family. She had rejected what she saw as an archaic process, with the rabbi or matchmaker suggesting a suitable marriage partner. Adherence to a strict protocol would then ensue, whereby the couple would meet under supervision and, if mutually agreeable, would meet again until a decision to marry followed shortly afterwards. Their doctrine was that love did not necessarily precede marriage, but once married you fell in love. In Miriam and Josh's case, Stuart, his best friend, was engaged to a sweet, thoughtful girl called Judy, a cousin of Miriam's. Knowing that Josh was a bit of a rebel himself, Judy had suggested introducing them.

Josh had resisted meeting Miriam, concerned that her family might be too great an influence, which would emphasize the divides in their religious commitment. Miriam's upbringing was very different from his. She had attended religious Jewish schools where the sexes were segregated at an early age. The focus at these schools was on Torah learning and studying the code of Jewish law, which governed every single aspect of their waking lives, from prayers and kashrut to laws surrounding purity.

One Sunday afternoon Josh had accompanied Stuart to visit Judy at her Maida Vale flat, which she shared with three other provincial girls. Their Sunday afternoon teas had become something of an institution. Friends would drop in for informal chats, heated debates or simply for the congenial company and tempting pastries made by the girls. Josh was intrigued when Stuart had related anecdotes from these gatherings and decided to join his friend one Sunday afternoon. Judy had persuaded her aunt to allow Miriam to come. Had her aunt known that the gathering included boys, she would not have allowed her daughter to go.

Miriam's father and Judy's mother were twins who had grown up in the strictly-orthodox community of Gateshead, famous for its yeshivas - houses of religious learning. Two siblings amongst a large brood, they had been extremely close when growing up, but could not have gone on to lead more dissimilar lives.

Miriam's father had married a strictly-orthodox girl from Stamford Hill, where they settled and happily raised their ever growing family. Judy's mother married a boy from an eminent Newcastle family. Leading a more relaxed Jewish lifestyle, they often attended Shabbat morning prayers in the synagogue, followed by a visit to St. James's football ground in the afternoon. They loved to dance and many Saturday nights were spent at their local club practicing the popular dances of the day, such as the Charleston and fox trot. Eventually they became professional dancers which horrified her brother and family, but despite these differences they still managed to remain close.

Miriam was a dainty, freckled redhead, and Josh warmed to her friendly chatter. At first, they would meet once a week at the Sunday afternoon gatherings in Maida Vale and then they began to date more often. Josh realised that he looked forward to seeing her. Was that love? At the time he assumed it must be and when she suggested getting married, he simply allowed himself to be carried along with the momentum.

Josh retrieved a memory of utter dread, on the day Miriam took him home to meet her parents. They had been cordial towards him, but made it very evident that they were not overjoyed at the match. Once they had made discreet inquiries and ascertained that Josh came from a highly respected family, they reluctantly accepted his presence, especially considering Miriam's rebellious tendencies. The fact that he was not as religious as they would have liked was, they felt, something that would change under their guidance and once children came along.

At first Miriam and Josh were totally compatible with their level of religion, but as he had initially feared, over the years the influencing factor of her family became evident. Gradually Miriam adhered to more and more stringencies, becoming rigidly fastidious over every detail of their lives and rituals. She refused to participate in anything that she considered frivolous.

Perhaps he should have given second thoughts to their marriage when discussions between their parents over wedding plans became heated, but by that stage he was so deeply entrenched that he never even considered calling it off. Miriam's family wanted separate seating for men and women in accordance with their practice. Josh's parents were extremely upset, knowing that their family and friends would be uncomfortable with this arrangement. After lengthy discourse a compromise was reached. Her family had separate tables for men and women, whilst his family had mixed seating for their guests. Another disturbing revelation for Josh was when Miriam told him that she would be accompanied to the marriage ceremony by both mothers, her face totally obscured by a thick white cloth instead of the conventional veil.

Indeed the wedding had been a fragmented affair.

The Gateshead family poured out of their hired coach into the wedding hall en-masse. After the ceremony the guests found their designated tables. One section of the wedding hall heaved with men gyrating together in wild joyous euphoria behind a thick curtain. Another area, equally well-shrouded, held the women also dancing, but with more reserve. A third section next to the band was allocated for Josh's family and friends to enjoy mixed dancing. Miriam had tactfully asked Judy to inquire whether her own parents would prefer to sit with her family, or in the mixed area. They had chosen to sit in the mixed area and had dazzled everyone with their skilful choreography.

As if the wedding plans had not been enough to contend with, there was also the issue of the honeymoon. Josh had taken it for granted that they would go away immediately after the wedding, but in this matter her family was adamant. The bride and groom must attend a week of sheva brachot, the seven blessings. Family and friends would continue to celebrate with the newlyweds for another week, in order to sanctify their marriage. The laws of niddah - family purity, forbade husband and wife from any physical contact in the days following consummation of the marriage. Therefore, these daily festivities served as a diversion.

Despite his apprehensions, the week of sheva brachot sped by with truly joyous gatherings. Sumptuous meals were hosted each evening by a different friend or family member. They agreed to defer their honeymoon for a few weeks and when they did go, they spent two weeks touring

Ireland in perfect marital harmony. Away from the strictures of her family, Miriam had been happy-go-lucky and relaxed, but that would gradually change

With the arrival of each child Josh became aware of some disturbing developments. Although undiagnosed at the time, Miriam suffered from postnatal depression which deteriorated with each subsequent birth. She hid it from her family and friends, fearing stigma and disgrace. Only Josh knew about her dreadful bouts of depression. Her misery was palpable, but because of her adamant refusal to seek help Josh felt powerless. She simply became more and more devout, insisting that this was her solace. Eventually Josh did speak to a friend who was a therapist and Miriam agreed to begin treatment which helped alleviate her difficult days.

By now, the carefree girl he had married had gradually turned into an unyielding, matronly figure who adhered to the strictest interpretation of the law, chastising him for every iniquity. She would reprimand him on Shabbat if she caught him picking the beans out of his cholent because that was sorting, or if he tore across the writing when he opened a packet of biscuits. She would even check to ensure that he had been scrupulous about his prayers.

For the sake of the children Josh tried to conform with her demands and constraints, agreeing to send them to strictly-orthodox schools. He was not even aware that he wasn't content, it was simply life. Once he had crossed the line together with Yang, he knew his perspective of life could never go back to what it had been. He often thought about a quote from his hero Sir Winston Churchill.

"*Men occasionally stumble over the truth, but most of them pick themselves up and hurry off as if nothing had happened.*" Josh had inadvertently stumbled over his own truth and now he could never pretend otherwise.

Emerging from his ruminations, he knew he was pursuing an ill-conceived quest. In the morning he would apprise Alistair of his decision not to continue his search.

Chapter Four

"You can fool some of the people all of the time,
and all of the people some of the time,
but you can't fool all of the people all of the time."
Abraham Lincoln

Wednesday 30th October 2019. Shanghai

Josh's personal concerns were all but forgotten when he discovered a distraught Alistair waiting for him at breakfast. Barely able to control his feelings, Alistair told Josh that he had just overheard a very distressing conversation.

'Two hotel clerks were conversing in Chinese and obviously assumed that I would not understand. Apparently a famous French model has committed suicide in one of the hotel bedrooms. She was discovered by the chambermaid who was in a state of total shock, after entering the room and finding her hanging from the chandelier suspended by a few silk scarves. Seemingly the poor woman stood on a chair then kicked it away. The management of the hotel are obviously keen to maintain a silence on it, as this is certainly not the sort of exposure a hotel of this calibre would welcome.'

'It's lucky for them that you are not an unscrupulous newspaper reporter.' Josh observed.

He had by now perceived that Alistair, being a sensitive soul, sometimes even prone to histrionics, needed a diversion before his tears became evident.

'Where are you taking me today?' he enquired. Promptly distracted, Alistair responded with his typically erudite flair. 'We'll start at the Children's Palace and then there are a multitude of fascinating sites to enliven our senses.'

During the drive, Alistair gave Josh some background on The Children's Palace.

'It was owned by the Kadoorie family and known as the "*Marble Hall*". When it was built in 1924 it was considered one of the most elegant stately homes in Shanghai. It is now used by the China Welfare Institute, and after school classes are given in a multitude of different subjects including dance, music and acrobatics. During World War Two, the Japanese put some of the Kadoories into a detention camp and the house was requisitioned. Despite this, the Kadoorie descendants, knowing that their family's former home is being put to such good use, have stated their gratification.'

In spite of Alistair's build-up, Josh was still awed by the elaborate and ornate grandeur of it all. The rooms were adorned with white Italian marble walls, columns and fireplaces, whilst crystal chandeliers hung from festooned ceilings. In one of the largest rooms, which must have served in its time as a ballroom, they watched a ballet class in progress. Josh was struck by the flawlessly synchronized formation of these little girls, who could not have been more than five years old. There must have been forty girls in identical pink dresses, all dancing with astonishing coordination. It was obvious that they had been trained to attain perfection from an early age.

Walking along the Bund in the direction of the Yu Gardens, Alistair told Josh that they were originally built during the Ming dynasty as a private retreat for one family and were designed according to the philosophy of Feng Shui. As they entered, Josh was struck by the soothing effect of the layout and unexpectedly Yang's words crept into his head. She had described Feng Shui to him as an energy force which harmonizes individuals with their environment. Seeing such a perfect example, he was now able to understand it. Rarely had he encountered such peace, conveyed through the tranquillity of foliage, rockery, ponds and pavilions.

Their tour, which would have been incomplete without a visit to the famous Nanjing Road, didn't go as smoothly as planned. A teeming mass of people were walking in all directions. Alistair and Josh had just left the pedestrianised zone, ambling along happily savouring their Haagen Daz ice creams, when inexplicably Josh found himself splayed on the road, a car narrowly managing to avoid him. Blood poured from his chin as Alistair helped him up, and onlookers came to offer assistance. Despite Josh's insistence that he was okay, blood still flowed out and the consensus was that he should be taken to the nearest hospital to be checked. Keeping a firm hold on his chin with a handkerchief proffered by an onlooker, they made their way to the nearest metro station, which Alistair thought would be the quickest mode of transport.

On the crowded platform a melee of bodies jostled, pushed or pressed against them. They heard the rumble of the approaching train and in that split second Josh felt the weirdest sensation, as if he was being propelled forward onto the line. Grabbing hold of Alistair in shock he gasped, 'I think I must be more lightheaded and wobbly than I thought.'

After an interminable delay in the emergency room of the hospital, they perceived that the only way to be seen was simply to join the crush of people crowding out the doctor's consulting room, placing Josh's file at the top of the pile on the desk. No one objected and Josh's wound, which was just superficial, received fast attention.

'What's going on?' Alistair enquired with concern once they were sitting quietly in the hospital cafe. 'Do you have a medical condition that I should know about?'

'Well, I know that I often allow the fantasies of my imagination to go too far, but I do believe in this instance that I was deliberately pushed from behind, both in the street and again at the station.'

'Surely not!'

'Let's just consider. 'If Yang's parents were involved in something suspicious then perhaps that address we went to is a front for something else. You said that you thought we were followed, so they would know where we are staying. If they have put us under surveillance they would know we have gone to an investigation agency. Perhaps this is their way of warning me to stop looking.'

On their return to the hotel, a message to call Mr. Wong from the investigation agency awaited them. 'Ah yes, Mr. Josh, Important information for you. Please come to my office tomorrow as there is also a small matter of fees to pay,' emphasizing the words "*to pay*" with his bizarre giggle.

Chapter Five

"I've learned that people will forget what you said,
people will forget what you did,
but people will never forget how you made them feel."
Maya Angelou

Thursday 31st October 2019. Shanghai

Mr. Wong greeted them warmly. 'I discover positive thing, yes! I do not find Yang, but parents live near the river in the town of Zhujiajiao, just an hour from here. I drive you there yes and I can try out new jokes on you.' Such personal service, in addition to listening to his appalling jokes, would be too much for Alistair to endure. He thanked Mr. Wong, but declined his kind offer, explaining that he was well acquainted with the area.

With this news, Josh's fears were quelled slightly and he put all disquieting and suspicious thoughts out of his mind. He had read about Zhujiajiao in his guide book, where it was dubbed the Venice of China. Known for its canals and classical gardens, Josh was happy that their excursions would take them there. He had also read about the Shanghai Jewish Refugees Museum, commemorating the story of some twenty thousand Jews who had fled Nazi Germany and were provided sanctuary in Shanghai. Josh was particularly curious to visit the museum, knowing that most of the world had closed their doors to these refugees. The tiny Dominican Republic was the only country to offer help, willing to take up to 100,000, but in the end a mere 700 were able to make it there. At the time Shanghai had been a multicultural oasis and since no entry visa was required, it offered these stateless refugees a beacon of hope. The Museum was not too far from their hotel so Alistair suggested they commence the day there, before driving on to the water town.

Entering the courtyard of the museum they were transfixed by the long copper memorial wall, engraved with more than thirteen thousand names of those saved, as well as a statue depicting their experience. As Josh looked at the alphabetical lists, he recalled a friend telling him that his father had lived in Shanghai during the war. Finding that family name on the wall sent a shiver down his spine.

They spent time viewing the artefacts and historical photos and reading about the plight of the refugees after their arrival in Shanghai. They were housed in the area of the Ohel Moshe Synagogue, where most of the city's Jewish community had resided. Both the Jews and Chinese suffered the ravages of war, but tried to help one another during the Japanese occupation. Josh and Alistair took a walk through the area covering approximately one square mile, which had been known as the restricted area or ghetto. It was hard to imagine the miserable living conditions those poor people had endured,

Josh had grown up with first-hand accounts of the Holocaust and ghetto life, so although greatly moved, was less shocked than Alistair, who was extremely subdued as they left to continue on their way.

Once Alistair regained his composure, he revealed that he was well acquainted with Zhujiajiao, as there were a number of snuff bottle dealers amongst the shops lining the bank of the canal.

Josh became increasingly apprehensive as they neared their destination, knowing that he was on a fool's errand. Locating the address, a small house close to the water's edge, there was no response to their knocking. Undeterred, Alistair tried the front door which was unlocked. Upon entering, Josh was astonished to see a large portrait of Yang on the wall. At least he knew they were in the right place.

Apparently the occupants were not around, so closing the door, they went in pursuit of refreshments. Wandering in and out of the shops running alongside the river, they found a kiosk which only served tea. Josh no longer complied scrupulously to dietary laws when he travelled abroad. Keeping to a vegetarian diet he would nevertheless eat in a non-kosher restaurant, which he knew was considered unacceptable in religious circles. Alistair, knowing well of the dangers lurking in meat consumption in China, was also extremely careful in his choice of food and restaurants.

Refreshed by the tea, they returned to the house where Josh was shocked by the sight of Yang's mother sitting outside in a wheelchair. She had aged considerably and looked extremely frail. She stared at Josh with a quizzical expression.

'It's me, Josh from Israel.' Her vacant expression didn't change. Just then another lady approached.

'Liat no talk, no understand.' She stated bluntly.

Outlining briefly that he had known Liat's daughter Yang when she lived in Israel, Josh explained that he merely wanted to look her up. Judging by the blank look on the woman's face, it was clear that her English did not extend to such dialogue.

Alistair translated into Chinese, provoking a torrent of words with occasional interjections from Alistair. Josh, assuming this lengthy exchange would shed some light on his search, was disappointed when Alistair summarized her responses.

'This is Chen, a neighbour who comes in every day to help. Yang has not been back for a long time and Chen has no idea of her present whereabouts. Before the stroke, Liat had told Chen that her daughter was living in a luxurious penthouse in Israel with a dashing billionaire lawyer.

Josh had to laugh at his dramatically inflated image.

Afterwards she changed her story, telling Chen that Yang had met a famous film star and moved to Beijing with him. Chen liked Sammy the amiable husband, but had always been wary of Liat and her implausible tales. Chen had never believed her, when she claimed that she had lived on an exclusive road in Shanghai, known for its affluent residents. When Liat had a stroke, Sammy offered to pay Chen a generous monthly salary to look after Liat. Despite her misgivings, Chen agreed to this arrangement and Sammy promptly disappeared, leaving her the name of his bank. Ever since then, the money has come in regularly.'

'So let's try the bank,' Josh suggested.

'Chen did make contact with the bank some time ago only to be told that they could not divulge any information about the source of the funds. Sorry Josh, but at this stage I doubt we can glean anything more from our visit.'

Josh persisted. 'Perhaps the reason she left me was connected to her mother's stroke. Can you ask her what year that was?'

'She says it was 2011.'

'Is she sure?'

'Absolutely, she remembers because it happened on September eleventh, 2011, the tenth anniversary of the Twin Tower attack.'

'So much for that theory Yang left me in November 2009.'

Thanking Chen for her help, Josh approached Liat and gently took her hand to say goodbye. As he did, he noticed the gold bracelet on her wrist. Taking a closer look, he recognised one of the charms attached to it; a tiny book, with the first words of each of the Ten Commandments engraved in Hebrew on a minuscule scroll. Josh was immediately transported back to the time he helped Yang choose it, as a birthday gift for her mother. It suddenly dawned on him with shock, that it was actually the last day they had ever spent together.

They had been at a jewellery stall in the sprawling Jaffa flea market. With crowds thronging to and fro, he had risked accompanying her through the multitude of narrow alleys, each one lined on both sides, with stalls offering a selection of colourful and kitschy items. Yang had been fascinated when she found the tiny gold talisman and Josh had pointed out the significance of the words. Choosing a pretty gold bracelet, they waited while the stall holder skilfully soldered it on.

'Alistair, please ask Chen where all the charms come from.'

'Apparently every year another one arrives on Liat's birthday. Chen takes the new charm to the jewellers to have it added to the bracelet, but there is never a return name or address on the package.'

While they thanked Chen and left a contact number in case she should hear from Yang, Josh counted the number of charms on the bracelet and was heartened to count ten. This was the first indication that Yang could be leading a life of normalcy and he became aware of his heart palpitating.

'I presume another one will be arriving shortly,' Josh muttered, knowing that Liat's birthday was at the end of November.'

Again Josh was taken back in time. As they were about to leave the stall with Yang clutching her prized purchase,

Josh was horrified to see the stall holder lift up a diamond ring, suggesting that he buy it for his charming young sweetheart. Yang regarded it with longing and gave Josh an imploring look as she said 'My mother's best birthday present would be to hear that we were engaged.' Without comment Josh hastily ushered her away.

Yang was still asleep when he left for the airport in the early hours, but he thought he had managed to diffuse the strained atmosphere, before they had retired to bed. He told her he loved her deeply and he knew that she deserved to be number one in his life, but this was all he was able to give of himself. There was no doubt, he emphasized, that she was number one in his heart. He promised to bring her a special gift back from London as a token of his everlasting love, which seemed to placate her. She had told him that she wished their situation could be different, but she understood and accepted it, because she couldn't imagine her life without him.

On the journey back to the hotel, Alistair apprised Josh of his own quest. He had been advised to continue the search for his snuff bottle in Beijing and hoped that Josh would accompany him, to continue pursuit of his own crusade.

Josh knew that Alistair had enjoyed their exploits together, that he was certainly a man of means and that he did not have a wife and children awaiting his return, but despite it all, Josh did not want to take advantage of Alistair's benevolent nature.

'Alistair, I appreciate how much you have helped me, but I can't take up more of your time, and I am not sure I even want to know that Yang has found happiness with some rich film star in Beijing.' Alistair looked crestfallen.

'The truth is that I've relished our times together, and was looking forward to continuing them in Beijing. Admittedly, it was a tenuous lead from Liat's neighbour, but why not come with me so that I can at least show you the Forbidden City. Maybe we can even climb the Great Wall together?'

Ever since Josh, as a schoolboy, had read about these extraordinary landmarks, they had held a fascination for him. To return to suburban Hendon without seeing them would indeed be a travesty of opportunity. How could he justify to his sixteen year old self that he had not taken a once in a lifetime opportunity to visit these historic sites? He also knew that he would not have ventured further had he been alone. As he nodded his acquiescence to Alistair's suggestion, he could see the look of happiness on his friend's face.

'Don't worry, I'll take care of the flights and hotel reservations and let's go tomorrow.'

Back in Mr. Wong's office, they reported the full details of their visit to the address he had given them. He promised to investigate further, to see if the bank would give him details on the whereabouts of Yang's father. When he heard they were traveling to Beijing he told them to contact his brother.

'He runs 'Kung Fu Investigation Agency there. He was ex-cop, a fall guy, so he has, how you say, certain cops still in his pocket. You will find him most efficient and helpful. Just another small fee to kindly pay me.'

Ultimately Josh knew that no good could come of this escapade. He would simply be opening a box on a life now closed to him. While he weighed up his options, Alistair was racing ahead.

'We must book our flights straight away.'

"The better I get to know men,
the more I find myself loving dogs."
Charles De Gaulle

Friday 1st November 2019. Beijing

The only flight Alistair had managed to book meant a very early morning start. In order to give himself plenty of time to pack, Josh set his alarm for 05:00 am. Always fastidious over his appearance, he carefully separated the dirty clothes from the clean, putting them into the laundry bag supplied by the hotel. As they were settling their bill, an official looking employee came over and whispered something to the clerk, who requested that Josh accompany him to a private room, together with his luggage. Frightening thoughts raced through his head as he recalled the numerous cases his law firm had dealt with over the years, incidents where innocent people were found with drugs in their baggage, having no idea where they came from. He was told to open his luggage where the purloined item, the laundry bag, was revealed and shamefully had to be relinquished. Josh was highly embarrassed by the incident which Alistair found most amusing.

'Sorry Josh I should have warned you that the Chinese are rather possessive over their laundry bags.'

During their two hour flight Josh asked Alistair about his own enquiries.

'From my sources in Shanghai it seems that the snuff bottle has not turned up there, but I've been given the name of a Beijing bigwig when it comes to the domain of shady dealings.'

'Sounds dangerous' Josh declared with concern.

'Don't worry,' Alistair replied resolutely 'I won't meet him in some secluded seedy venue; I'll insist he comes to the hotel. So now you have heard about my early years, what did you do in your misspent youth?' Alistair enquired.

'Hmm. Mine is a fairly uneventful story in comparison to your colourful life. The highlight of my fledgling years was probably my cycle accident.' Alistair looked at him expectantly for clarification.

'Well it was June 1962. I was speeding on my bike, because I was late for my bar-mitzvah lesson. Even back then my mind would go wandering off on excursions of its own, so I wasn't concentrating properly. I had just read about Moses Cohen Henriques, who was a Jewish pirate in the Caribbean and I was imagining myself as swashbuckling Captain Josh Henriques, sailing away on my ship for some high sea jinks. I didn't notice the lorry pulling out and I crashed into the back of it. I was thrown off the bicycle which came tumbling down on top of me. I do remember a lot of blood which seemed to be everywhere.

An ambulance was called, and if I hadn't been so worried that I might have incurred horrific injuries, not to mention the dreadful pain soaring throughout my body, being driven through the streets at breakneck speed with a siren blasting, could have been an awesome experience.

Initially, the ambulance headed towards the local hospital but as I drifted in and out of consciousness, I heard the medics say that my injuries might be too serious, so they decided to go directly to the Middlesex Hospital. Somehow I managed to mumble my home phone number and my anguished parents met me at the hospital, where I was promptly x-rayed. Fortunately the results showed that apart from a badly broken leg and lots of scrapes and bruises, my wounds were not as severe as first thought. My leg was broken in a couple of places and needed surgery, but nothing life-threatening.

After the operation I was put on a ward to recuperate for a few days. Once I could hobble about on crutches I would wander around. I had heard one nurse whisper the name Winston to another nurse, and although I thought it highly unlikely, I did wonder if she could possibly be talking about my hero, Sir Winston Churchill. I limped to the end of the ward, beyond which I could see a room cordoned off. Seizing the opportunity of a deserted corridor, I decided to slip past the roped off area and peer through the glass.

To my utter incredulity, there was the great man himself, sitting up in bed surrounded by papers. I was about to scuttle away as best I could when he saw me. To my even greater astonishment he beckoned me in.

"*Lad,*" he said "*do you see that cigar over there on the locker? Be a good fella and bring it here together with the packet of matches. They try to ration me to one cigar and one whiskey a day, but how can I make a recovery on such a meagre diet.*"

It was not an easy task for me, but I'd have thrown away my crutches and crawled if I had to, just to comply with his wishes. With some difficulty I managed to light his cigar, but then to my utter shame and horror, I dropped the lighted match on his papers. Fortunately, I managed to grab a towel next to his bed and smother the flames without too much damage. Quite unruffled, he laughed, tousled my hair and suggested I make a daily visit. At this time of day his minders were not present so I could repeat the favour, but preferably without the fire. As I nodded in agreement and went out, I turned back to wave and he gave me his famous V-sign.'

'What was he in the hospital for?'

'Whilst staying at the Hotel de Paris in Monte Carlo he fell out of bed and broke his hip. Adamant that he did not want to die abroad, he was flown back to London.

On my last day in hospital, I went in to tell him that I was leaving and he asked how I had been injured. When I regaled the whole sad story, he told me to pass him two cigars. He lit one and gave the other one to me, saying it was a bar-mitzvah present.'

'Do you still have it or did you smoke it?'

'It still has pride of place in my study.'

'Surely it has disintegrated by now.'

'No. Fortunately I inherited my father's humidor where it has been stored for the last fifty seven years. It was Winston's favourite brand, La Aroma de Cuba and quite different from the cigars my father smoked. Dad would often tease me and tell me that he had smoked it by mistake, but I knew he never would. He was as proud of my acquisition as I was.

Apart from that momentous encounter, my life in post-war Britain probably mirrors the lives of many people with vague recollections from the early fifties, such as rationing, playing hopscotch on the pavement and especially the thrill when their first television set arrived. Growing up with three older sisters I was always treated like the baby, but they did include me in the creative shows they organised, even if I was just their stooge. They were all quite talented and turned our garage into a little theatre, performing for friends and neighbours and then donating the proceeds to charity. Not quite up to Footlights standard but well enough for our neighbourhood.

Our dad was called Harry so they called themselves Harry's Little Angels. Jasmine would walk around on stilts dressed as a clown, handing out flyers informing people of an upcoming show. My parents gave us all names beginning with the letter J. My sisters are Jasmine, Juliette and Josephine. Juliette and Josephine both have superb singing voices so there was always music in the house as they sang popular songs of the day. At their shows they would sing, dance and tell jokes followed by Jasmine performing magic tricks.

I remember on one occasion Jasmine decided to use a live bird, which she was going to make disappear by magic. In order to advertise this performance, she prepared fliers with bird illustrations surrounding the words *live bird.* She went to the pet shop and came home proudly carrying a birdcage, containing a sad looking dove with bedraggled feathers. Just before the show was due to start, Juliette declared that the bird was too scruffy and she was going to give it a wash. I offered to help and we took the birdcage outside. As Juliette was about to open the door of the cage I asked "she won't fly away will she?" to which Juliette replied "no she can't, she has been clipped." The moment she opened the door, this bird with clipped wings soared out of the cage and flew upwards, perching on the ledge of my bedroom window. We rushed up to my room and stealthily opened the window. Juliette made a grab for the bird but it took off again, this time gliding up to the sky.'

'So it really did do a disappearing act' Alistair commented with amusement.

'Yes and we had to break the news to Jasmine. Losing the bird was bad enough, but she had done such a good job publicizing the event that our garage was filling up with more and more people arriving the whole time. Juliette told Jasmine and as you can imagine it wasn't a pretty scene. In the end I found an old stuffed bird in my toy cupboard and she had to use that.'

'Did people ask for their money back?'

'I think they might have done, but as it was for charity no one could really complain. Anyway Juliette and Josephine made up a funny comedy sketch to illustrate the bird's escape.'

'Where did you all go to school?'

'We all went to the local primary school. I went on to Haberdashers, where I also played rugby and also hated it. Most of my local friends attended synagogue on Shabbat morning, some complying more strictly with the Shabbat laws, others less so, some kept kosher, others were more lax. In some ways it was like going to a supermarket and choosing the appropriate items necessary for your life.

Most of us tried to conform out of respect for our parents, but at the same time we wanted to participate in the vibrancy and energy of the era. I had a separate group of friends from school and we would all meet up and go to a club or dance over the weekend. In some ways I tried to run with the hare and hunt with the hounds, in order to keep up with my friends while trying at the same time to live up to my parent's religious values. I guess that has been the story of my life.

We didn't appreciate it at the time when we were coming of age, but the swinging sixties was probably one of the most significant decades in Britain's history. The country was emerging from the austerity of the war and its aftermath, into a vibrant and exciting climate.'

'Unfortunately my rites of passage into manhood were suppressed in Brunei and then stifled further at Rugby School, so I missed out on most of the fun-loving hedonism of the sixties and early seventies. I did manage to make my own amusement though. Did I ever tell you my dog story when I was living in Brunei?'

'No' Josh responded, settling back to be regaled by one of Alistair's vivid narratives.

'Well, despite the fact that dogs are not over popular in Brunei since it is a Muslim country, my father bought me one for companionship as he recognized my loneliness. I am now about to depict the scene of my finest hour.

It is my mother's turn to host her weekly bridge game at our palatial Brunei residence, or as I called it "Bleak House". Sixteen prim and proper ladies arrive, finely and fashionably attired and are shown into the card room, which is decorated to perfection in baroque style grandeur. My mother greets her guests with decorous formality and invites them to take their seats at the four card tables set out with playing cards, score markers and pencils. Half way through the proceedings, they break for tea. The ladies are cordially invited to sit round the dining table, which is resplendent with a selection of cakes and biscuits.

This was the only time I was allowed into the kitchen to help the cook. I loved baking and would make my favourite chocolate chip cookies for the occasion. Unbeknown to anyone, I had exchanged a few of my cookies for some dog biscuits which bore a remarkable resemblance to the real thing. Hiding behind the door, I watched as these demure ladies with impeccable manners and stilted decorum tried to chew these indigestible biscuits. Unfortunately, my whoops of joy could be heard from behind the door, and my mother, white with fury, emitted an uncharacteristic scream of horror, as she ran out of the room and caught me by the ear. As she dragged me back into the room, she told the gathered assembly that she could not fathom how a child of hers could be the author of such a cruel and heartless prank. My mother saw it as my complete downfall, whereas I thought I showed great ingenuity. Funny how two people can see the same situation from totally different viewpoints. Despite the punishment meted out, it did not diminish one of my best childhood moments.'

Thanks to their recollections the two hour flight to Beijing seemed to flash by and once landed, Alistair steered Josh out of the airport and into a waiting cab. Josh was feeling quite laid back, leaving all the arrangements to Alistair, who was plainly on familiar terrain.

After settling into their hotel and grabbing a quick breakfast, they headed outside and hailed a taxi to Tiananmen Square where thousands of people were congregating. Finding a group with an English speaking guide, they tagged along. The guide informed them that they were standing in one of the largest city squares in the world, which unbelievably could accommodate three million people. Diplomatically, she omitted to mention the 1989 Tiananmen Square protests, when civilians were violently suppressed by the military and there were many deaths.

She then proceeded to lead them through the Rostrum into the famed Forbidden City. Was he really here, Josh kept asking himself, as he listened in fascination to the guide's narrative? He could never have visualized the enormity of this complex, which served as the winter residence of Chinese Emperors and their households, starting with the Ming dynasty in 1368 right through till the end of the Qing dynasty in 1912.

Leading her group through the many narrow paths, the guide swamped them with a multitude of facts and figures, relating that The Forbidden City is considered one of the most expensive pieces of real estate in the world. Despite being fascinated, Josh could feel his mind beginning to wander as they ventured deeper and deeper into the palace area, and then suddenly he became conscious that he had somehow separated from Alistair and the rest of the group. He looked around, but did not recognize anyone amongst the throng of humanity which crowded the space around him. The extent of his predicament hit him, when he attempted, but failed to remember the name of his hotel. After all, he had left all the booking arrangements to Alistair. To compound matters, his phone was not connected to a local network. He walked on in the direction he had last seen the group, frantically looking around for any sign of Alistair, but he knew it was futile. He decided to return to the main Tiananmen gate in the hope that he might find him, but even there the crowds were so dense, it was an impossible task.

Josh was not a man prone to panic. He had managed to extricate himself from some very difficult and even embarrassing situations over the years, but now felt a great chasm of dread accompanied by a sense of foreboding. Out of the hundreds of hotels in Beijing, how on earth was he going to find the one they were staying at? Taking deep slow breaths to try and compose himself, he decided to look through his wallet to see if by chance he had picked up the hotel card. All he found was the piece of paper from Mr. Wong with the name and address of their Beijing office. This was his only hope. He would find a taxi to take him to that address.

After what seemed like an eternity, he managed to flag an empty taxi, only to find that the driver did not understand a word of English. Fortunately for Josh, the piece of paper also had the address written in Chinese. On seeing it, the driver gave a nod of perception and sped off.

Twenty minutes later they turned into a deserted street and the driver pointed to a dilapidated structure which gave an appearance of eerie abandonment. Paying the taxi driver who raced off at breakneck speed, Josh opened the rusty steel door with great trepidation and ventured inside. He began to fear that the property was totally disused, as he opened one door after another, only to find gloomy rooms long forsaken.

Alone, in an old ramshackle construction, on an abandoned street in Beijing, with no idea as to the name of his hotel, he was becoming increasingly nervous and despondent. Throughout his life he had always managed to come up with a strategy, but at this precise moment he was totally stumped. Retracing his steps, he emerged through the door, wandering aimlessly along uneven paving stones, electric cables hanging dangerously low. A ghostly desolation pervaded the whole area. The roads were littered with rubble and broken furniture was strewn around haphazardly. Windows were boarded up and debris was scattered everywhere. The road came to a sudden end and he found himself walking down a stiflingly dark alleyway. He thought he heard footsteps behind him but was too nervous to look back. Was this where he was going to meet his demise? As he turned a corner, he glanced behind him but could see no one. Even here, his hyperactive imagination was playing tricks on him. He emerged from the alley into another derelict street where walls were covered in graffiti, mostly in an ugly scrawl. Adverts in English offered fake identities, guns, knives and other such valuable services. He noticed a tractor depicted in yellow paint with the words "demolition site" written next to it. The whole area was indeed only fit for bulldozing.

Josh decided to retrace his steps and found himself outside the original address. As he looked up, he thought he saw a figure peering out of a first floor window. With this last vestige of hope, he pushed open the rusty door again and climbed the creaking stairs. At the very end of the corridor he saw a sign in English displaying the words *Investigation Agency.*

To his great relief he was greeted by a Mr Wong look-alike when the door opened. 'Do you speak English?' Josh asked.

'Of course, finest investigation agency must speak finest English. Please excuse broken place. They pull down next week. With a rush of words Josh detailed his predicament.

'So you wish me to find hotel where you stay?' This might be possible, you registered yes? Please relax, you not look healthy, you very white. I make you cup of tea then I phone my contacts to see if they can help. I used to be policeman so I have important friends in police force.'

Overtaken by sheer exhaustion, Josh began to doze to the sound of the Mr Wong look-alike talking in animated Chinese. With a triumphant smile, he told Josh he had managed to find his name registered at the Manfulou Hotel. No wonder I couldn't remember the name Josh thought to himself as he thanked him effusively.

'Now, before I call taxi, anything else I can help with? You must have problem if you visit our office in Shanghai.' Against his better judgement, Josh found himself being drawn, yet again, to look inside that box which he thought he had sealed, by repeating the whole story of Yang's background and disappearance. Although he admonished his own weakness, he had not prevented a profusion of evocative images flooding back, as he had drifted in and out of awareness.

'Please give me all details you have and I see what I can find. I also speak to my brother in Shanghai and we work together. Now just small fees, then I call taxi to take you safely back to hotel.'

Josh was overcome with gratitude when he drew up at the hotel and saw Alistair standing outside, with a look of grave concern on his face. That look turned into an enormous smile when he saw Josh emerging unscathed.

'Oh Josh my friend I am so sorry we were separated' he said as he embraced him in a bear hug. Alistair could not hide his genuine concern, as he told him that he had spent the rest of the day searching for him.

When Josh returned to his room he made the obligatory call to Miriam. He knew she would be at home preparing meals. He couldn't remember which children and grandchildren had messaged him to say that they would be visiting her, but no matter, the cholent, the traditional Shabbat meal, always seemed to stretch. He knew it was a good time to call, since Shabbat had not yet commenced in China and the UK was 8 hours behind. Yes, he told her, work was going well and he would be home before too long. Well-practiced in deception by omission, he deluded himself that he wasn't really lying. Her only concern was indeed how he would be sanctifying the day. Had he arranged for kosher meals? Where would he be praying? How would he open his bedroom door without using the electronic card? Which floor was he on since obviously, he wouldn't be using the lift? 'Don't worry it's all sorted out' he replied, adding with conviction that he must rush because Shabbat would be starting shortly.

Chapter Seven

"By all means marry. If you get a good wife, you'll become happy; if you get a bad one, you'll become a philosopher."
Socrates.

Saturday 2nd November 2019. Beijing

Over the years Josh had become lax over certain rigours of the religion; however the rich heritage, the wealth of customs and traditions, the beauty of the festivals each with their own distinctive ceremonial artefacts, were all an indispensable component of his life. Some elements were simply second nature to him, so fundamental that he performed them automatically. He was stringent about wearing his tzitzit, the knotted fringes attached to the four corners of a garment resembling a vest. He remembered how Yang used to make fun of him when he put them on every morning. Despite their intimacy, it was one thing he would never allow her to touch; it would have seemed sacrilegious to him, as if it would diminish their sanctity. He also refrained from traveling on Shabbat, so asked Alistair if there was somewhere interesting within walking distance,

Alistair told him he had specifically chosen this inauspicious hotel with its unmemorable name, so that they were within an easy walk of the famous Zhongshan Park.

Not only was it an enchanting park with scenic gardens, it was also a popular weekend venue for thousands of parents and grandparents. They gathered in an attempt to find a suitable marriage partner for their son or daughter. Josh was fascinated to learn more, because it sounded not so far removed from the Haredi approach, where parents were paramount in choosing a suitable match for their children.

Approaching the park, they beheld the sight of hundreds of colourful umbrellas open on the ground, each one with a foolscap page of writing pinned to it. Although the hopeful parents or grandparents would be relaxing some distance back from the umbrellas, they would be maintaining a keen surveillance on the scene for the approach of a possible match. Alistair expounded that each page contained personal details of the prospective bride or groom such as age, appearance, house ownership, family background, education and anything else relevant, apart from a photograph.

'Also included,' Alistair continued, 'are the contact details of the parents, or in many cases the grandparents. Family often plays a key role in arranging marriages and China's one child policy also meant a one grandchild policy. Very often the children have no idea that their details are displayed publicly and would probably be mortified if they knew. It all started in 2004 when a group of parents gathered in this very park. Instead of bemoaning the single status of their children, they decided to do something about it. Since then it has mushroomed and is now a popular weekly event in the parks of many big cities. The status of marriage is considered very important in Chinese life and if a child is still single by his or her mid-twenties, they are often viewed as *leftovers*.'

As Alistair was talking, Josh noticed a cameraman with a BBC sign, and a lady trying to interview some of the parents, but they all covered their faces or turned away.

'They are frightened that their children will see them,' Alistair pointed out. The reporter had more success when she interviewed a prospective groom. He told her that he had been coming to the park for months, but sadly, had not found a parent or even a grandparent willing to consider him. They were all very particular and had told him quite bluntly that he was some combination of too small, too fat, too uneducated and too old.

Standing close by, Josh and Alistair could hear the interviewer probing further into his life. She then turned to Alistair and Josh, poised to interview them. Josh hastily moved away, horrified to think that he could be caught on camera, on a Shabbat, in a Chinese marriage-market, but not before he heard the reporter say *'Alistair?'* in an incredulous voice. From a safe distance Josh watched while Alistair held an intimate conversation with her. A few minutes later when Alistair re-joined him Josh asked how she knew him. 'Oh from my double act days' he replied evasively, uncharacteristic of his usual effusive openness.

Understanding that Alistair did not wish to pursue the conversation, Josh enquired if he knew of any successful matches made in this way.

'As it happens, I do. I've a friend, Chang, whom I met a few years ago when I took a course in the art of Gong Fu tea-making. He was the instructor and we have remained good friends since then. He managed to find a suitable match for his son through this approach.

The parents or grandparents are usually here without the permission of the child, and this was the case with my friend. His son Jan was always too busy to meet anyone, but was still very angry when his father found someone who sounded an ideal match. Jan refused to meet her, and she was similarly angry over her family's intervention, but Chang was persistent. He managed to procure a photo with her details and artfully left it where Jan was sure to see it. Jan relented and agreed to meet her and has since had to admit, his father found him the perfect match. The wedding took place shortly afterwards and they now live together with Chang and his wife, who are on hand to look after their granddaughter.

In fact, since they don't live far away I told Chang we might visit them for a Gong Fu tea ceremony, which is a very skilful ritual for the preparation and serving of tea. The method is intricate and Chang was an excellent teacher.' Josh was fascinated.

'You mean to say that it takes a whole course of lessons just to learn how to make a cup of tea?'

'Not just any tea' Alistair exclaimed in exaggerated horror. 'The ritual is also known as Kung Fu which is a whole philosophy, similar to mastering a martial art.' Curious at the prospect of such a visit, Josh readily agreed. Slightly further away than anticipated, they arrived at a complex secured by wrought iron gates, manned by a security guard. Once their credentials had been approved, they were permitted inside the labyrinth of winding paths and courtyards, passing gazebos, outdoor lounge areas and exercise equipment. When they arrived at their destination and were ushered inside, it was clear that the whole family were thrilled to see Alistair.

The tea ceremony was indeed complicated and elaborate. The matching cups, jug and teapot were displayed on an attractive latticework rack, sitting atop a hollow tray to catch the spills. A painstaking procedure then ensued, with boiling water poured into the cups before being emptied out over the tray. Tea leaves were measured carefully into the teapot and more boiling water was poured over the shoulder of the pot and on its lid, before the tea leaves were immersed. The ceremony progressed until at last the tea was ready for tasting. They sat quietly imbibing the fragrant brew and savouring the silence. The serenity was occasionally punctuated with the sound of slurping, which Josh presumed must indicate their enjoyment and appreciation.

When they left amidst warm farewells, Alistair asked Josh if he had enjoyed the tea. 'Would you be appalled if I said I loved the ceremony but still prefer Typhoo!'

As they walked back through the park, a bride and groom were being photographed in striking red costumes. Alistair pointed out that in China red is a symbol of happiness, so a bride and groom would often wear red costumes, later changing into western-style clothing, the bride wearing a conventional white dress. 'It is also traditional to have a tea ceremony at the wedding. The bride and groom serve their future in-laws with tea, as a symbol of a union not only between the couple, but also to signify the unification between the families.'

'You know,' Josh mused as they sauntered slowly back to the hotel, 'It seems to me that the Jewish and Chinese people share some basic values. In both cases, the custom of uniting over family meals encourages stronger connection, through frequent gatherings. In fact, this emphasis on staying together is probably a major force in the survival of both, for thousands of years.'

'Absolutely,' Alistair agreed. 'So a Chinese guy and a Jewish guy were talking about their histories and their traditions. The Chinese guy says "Chinese culture is more than three thousand years old" and he lists some of its achievements. The Jewish guy acknowledges China's rich history and says "Jewish culture is more than five thousand years old." The Chinese guy then interjects "no way, whatever did you eat for the first two thousand years." Sorry, the best joke I could come up with.'

'Nearly as bad as Mr. Wong's Josh replied.

Back at the hotel, Alistair pointed out an advert for the Golden Mask Dynasty show later that evening. 'This is one of the most spectacular performances I've ever seen, not to be missed and a must as part of your Beijing experience. I'll book tickets.'

Alistair had insisted that it was his treat and Josh had no doubt that he had purchased the most expensive seats, in the third row of the impressive theatre. As it filled up, Josh was puzzled to see that the two front rows remained unoccupied, but the reason soon became apparent. The show opened with a large number of dancers appearing in colourful costumes and a backdrop of a spectacular waterfall. Water actually cascaded over the stage, overflowing onto the first two rows of seats, under which were hidden drains. The whole theatre was aglow with luminous shadows and subdued lighting, creating an unearthly aura. Indeed, it was an evening of energetic, unrelenting entertainment. Kung Fu demonstrations, acrobatics and captivating song and dance routines, all accompanied by special effects and music befitting the scene. When the curtain fell, Josh told Alistair he was quite drained from the exhilaration of the whole experience.

"After climbing a great hill, one only finds that there are many more hills to climb."
Nelson Mandela

Sunday 3rd November 2019. Beijing

'Are you feeling fit today?' Alistair greeted Josh at breakfast.
'Why, what do you have in mind?'
'To climb the Great Wall,' Alistair replied with a hopeful expression on his face. Again Josh felt that he could not let down his sixteen year old self, who had often climbed the Great Wall in his dreams.

They poured over a map which showed the extensive length of the Wall, with Alistair pointing out the best access points. After careful deliberation, they agreed to make their way to the section closest to Beijing, despite this route having the steepest climb to the summit.

There was a feeling of camaraderie amongst the odd assortment of people starting out at the foot of the Great Wall. Some were strolling; some were striding, but all seemed to share the same objective, to reach the watchtower at the top, via the uneven steps snaking through the undulating countryside. It seemed natural to fall into conversation with strangers as they passed, with a nod or exchange of some pleasantries. An English couple were sharing facts from a guide book and were incredulous to read about the Wall's sheer length and age. As the ascent became more strenuous with steeper gradients, they stopped for a rest at the side of a rampart which was already occupied by a lady of indeterminate years, wearing bizarrely colourful attire.

She peered out from under an enormous hat, and wheezed in a strong American accent 'Gee am I glad to see you boys. Do you by any chance have some water? I didn't expect it to be such thirsty work.' Revived by their water, she stunned them with her directness.

'You know, I really do admire you two. Mind if I ask you something personal?'

Josh was used to people asking his age, so was totally taken aback when she asked 'how long have you boys been together? I am staying at the same hotel as you in Beijing. I happened to be coming into the hotel yesterday and I saw you embracing each other so lovingly outside the entrance. Then at breakfast I couldn't help but notice, you were both so intimately engrossed in conversation.'

As Josh stumbled over his protestations, Alistair gave him a wink and with an overtly effeminate gesture said 'Yes isn't it enchanting, we are celebrating our 30th togetherness anniversary.'

'Ah gee, that is so romantic. Me, three times married and none of them worked out. Next time I think I'll go down your path and find myself a gal. I wish you strength for the rest of your climb, I'm afraid I can't go on.'

With that she turned to descend the steps. Josh wanted to be cross with Alistair, but was becoming accustomed to his theatrics. Seeing the look of mirth on his face, Josh couldn't help but laugh. Climbing even more steeply, they reached the watchtower. They were rewarded by a panoramic view, as well as a gift shop where they could purchase a medal, to prove that they had made it to the pinnacle.

A message to call the Beijing Investigation Agency awaited Josh at the hotel. Later in bed, he deliberated over the advisability of calling. In his heart he knew he shouldn't. Thanks to Alistair he was having a remarkable holiday, so the trip was certainly not wasted. Alistair had even suggested they take the bullet train to Xian the next day to see the Terracotta Warriors. Yes, he decided as he drifted off to sleep, he wouldn't call the agency and they would go to Xian.

Invariably after a night's sleep things look different. When Josh awoke he realised that it was only polite to return the call.

'I find someone by name and description you give me but very little information,' Mr. Wong look-alike informed Josh. 'She was registered as full time student, studying piano at the music conservatory in Beijing nine years ago.'

'Piano,' Josh responded in amazement. 'I very much doubt that would be Yang as she was so focused on being a lawyer.' The moment he put the phone down he had a sudden flashback to the day when he heard her play the piano.

He had just walked into the Tel Aviv train station on his way home. Since the day she had moved into his flat he had been insistent that they never leave work together, never arrive together and were never seen on the train together. As he went further into the station he could hear the strains of a melody he recognized as the Turkish March by Mozart. The playing was quite mesmerising. Drawing closer, he joined a crowd gathered round the piano in the station forecourt and to his utter astonishment; he saw that it was Yang playing. He waited until she was almost finished and then hurried off to catch his train.

When she arrived home some time later, he revealed that he had heard her playing and expressed his admiration at her virtuosity. She told him that China's one-child policy meant that parents expected excellence from their offspring. All their resources were poured into ensuring that this should be so. In her case it was learning to play the piano and she simply hadn't thought to mention it. Recalling this, Josh resolved to call the agency on their return from Xian, as his curiosity was now aroused. Could she have possibly abandoned law, to become a professional pianist?

Chapter Nine

"It is never too late to be what you might have been"
George Elliot

Monday 4th/Tuesday 5th November 2019. Xian and Luoyang

The aptly named bullet train to Xian provided glimpses of largely uninhabited areas. Running at a speed of 250 to 300 kilometres an hour, it raced across the countryside, giving an impressive window on the real China. They passed mountains, forests and rice paddies, with tiny villages flashing by across a largely bleak landscape. Josh gazed out of the window fascinated by the illuminating view of Chinese life in microcosm. The train sped past the scene before he could even verbalize 'Alistair! Look.'

Despite the luxury and comfort of their first-class carriage, they were both tired after five hours on the train, agreeing to meet at breakfast before going to visit the famous site. Sixteen year-old Josh had been quite fascinated by Frank Kafka's short story about the Great Wall of China. At that stage in his life the Terracotta Warriors had not yet been uncovered. They were unearthed some years later by a group of peasants digging a well. Fragments of a clay figure turned out to be one of several thousand, thus exposing an extraordinary hidden treasure.

As they entered the Museum of the Terracotta Warriors, which was actually a huge exhibition erected around the discovery site, Josh was enthralled by the sight of countless long columns of reconstructed warriors and horses, standing in formation in massive pits.

The landscaped campus told two parallel stories and as they continued to a second pit, they saw how the soldiers had looked when originally found. They spent a long time just taking in the magnitude and magnificence of it all.

Their original plan had been to return to Beijing directly on the bullet train but Alistair asked Josh if he would object to a stop at Luoyang en-route. The missing snuff bottle had been purchased from a particular dealer there, who Alistair held in high esteem and was sure would help if possible.

'In addition,' Alistair added, 'Luoyang was one of the greatest ancient capitals, so it would be another fascinating place to visit.'

Naturally, Josh had no objection. In fact the more he saw of China, especially with the benefit of Alistair's formidable knowledge, the more he wanted to see. If only he could have shared all this with Miriam, perhaps their lives together would have been very different.

'How far is it?' Josh asked.

'By bullet train it takes about two hours and by slow train, probably four.'

'So why don't we take the slow train there, just to savour the countryside more gradually, then take the bullet train back to Beijing.'

After buying tickets and passing stringent security checks, they settled into their seats. Just as the doors were closing, two girls in their late teens clambered on with their suitcases. Alistair gallantly stood up to help them, as they struggled to put them in the overhead rack. Sitting opposite Josh and Alistair, their chirpy high-pitched Chinese chattering and giggling began to grate on Alistair as the train wended its way. He was trying to concentrate on the book he was reading, but their conversation caught his attention. One girl asked the other 'which one of these two old fellas would you fancy?'

Her companion replied, 'well the guy on the left looks like he's way past it and the other one looks like he wouldn't be interested at all.' Alistair tried to look nonchalant, as they elaborated amidst more giggles of hilarity. 'I bet we could teach them a thing or two.' They were obviously enjoying themselves, as they joked at Alistair and Josh's expense, discussing ludicrous antics and undreamt of contortions they could perform with their limbs and bodies.

Alistair wrote a note to Josh, giving the gist of their conversation and advising him not to look at the girls.

When they arrived in Luoyang Alistair helped the girls with their luggage. As he put the bags down on the platform he spoke in fluent Chinese.

'Please give us your address so we can come over and enjoy every detail of your spectacular manoeuvres.' The look of utter horror on their faces was only matched by the girls' screaming, as they picked up their cases and streaked down the platform. Josh and Alistair could hardly contain their laughter, watching them scamper away.

The entrance to the dealer's emporium was accessed via a pathway, hidden behind an ancient door. Upon entering, Josh was fascinated to see the collections of artefacts including many snuff bottles. Judging by their reception, Josh gathered that Alistair was a highly valued customer.

The dealer was obviously disturbed to hear about his lost snuff bottle, but could give no insight into its whereabouts. He would however be happy to show Alistair another snuff bottle recently acquired, which was painted in the same series. In fact, he had intended to contact Alistair to tell him about it. Alistair could not disguise his eagerness as it was slowly and laboriously unwrapped. His gasp of ecstasy was an indication of his admiration, while he examined it meticulously. Although Josh could not understand the ensuing conversation, staggering amounts were being bandied about in English, with negotiations flying back and forth. Josh was astounded by the original price asked by the dealer. Alistair on the other hand, was undaunted and totally satisfied when they came to a mutually agreeable compromise.

It was getting late and with no opportunity so far to see the rest of Luoyang, they decided to stay overnight. Before heading back to Beijing on the bullet train, they would devote the next day to sightseeing.

Later, relaxing in his hotel bedroom, a disquieting thought crossed Josh's mind. Alistair, with his latest acquisition might now consider returning home, despite his lack of progress on the disappearance of his original bottle.

Josh felt a distinct pang of sadness and disappointment at the prospect.

Chapter Ten

"Marriage is a wonderful institution.....
But who wants to live in an institution?"
Groucho Marx

Wednesday 6th November 2019. Longmen Grottoes

Meandering leisurely through the old city the next day, Alistair enlightened Josh on Luoyang's history. 'It was one of the four great ancient capitals of China throughout nine dynasties and is considered a cradle of Chinese civilization,'

Continuing his running commentary during their bus journey to the Longmen grottoes, Alistair told Josh about the phenomenal vision they were about to behold. 'The site was hailed on the UNESCO World Heritage list as an outstanding manifestation of human artistic creativity.'

When they alighted from the bus the reason for that acclaim was evident.

Running along both sides of the river bank, thousands of Buddha statues were crafted into the rock formation. Each niche contained sculptured images, some slightly weathered but still easily visible. More than two thousand three hundred caves were carved into the steep limestone cliffs, stretching for more than a kilometre. In the largest cave a regal statue stood seventeen meters high, surrounded by inscriptions.

'The writing explains the details of the carving,' Alistair elaborated. 'There were probably more than one hundred thousand statues carved during a period of four hundred years, some as small as ten centimetres and many others as high as this one.'

They climbed higher and higher, hardly noticing the effort involved, in order to admire the ancient structures from the best vantage point, but suddenly tiredness overcame them. Looking for a place to rest, they spotted a convenient bench with just one occupant. They were astounded when they heard a familiar American voice greet them.

'Well well, if it isn't the lover boys. In my country we have a saying, third time ice-cream, which means that if we bump into each other a third time, you have to buy me ice-cream.' She shuffled along the seat to make room.

'*Pa'am shlishit glidah*' Josh repeated the expression in Hebrew. 'As far as I know, it is an expression singular to Israel. Do you live there?' he asked.

'Yeah, despite looking like an American, sounding like an American and my name being Rica, I went to live in Israel twenty years ago when I was 24. You know what they say, you can take the gal out of America, but you can't take America out of the gal.'

Barely taking breath, Rica launched into her life story. 'I met my first husband singing in the choir at Temple

Shalom when I was twenty, married very shortly afterwards and divorced a year later. He turned out to be a sadist. Christian Grey had nothing on him! Then I met an Israeli who seemed to be perfect, handsome, kind and rich. We went to live in Eilat because he owned a construction company there. Everything was wonderful, until I found him in bed with his male masseur. Not that I've anything against being gay' she added hastily. 'I just didn't want to be married to one. I worked for him in his sales department and stayed on after our divorce. Fortunately it was all very amicable. You'd think I should have learnt to be more discerning by the time it came to picking husband number three, but no. Turned out he had been in prison for defrauding his ex-wife out of millions. Anyway, I stayed in Eilat and I still work in my second husband's business. What do you think of this place? I'm totally overawed by it. Can I offer you some water this time? You really saved me at the Great Wall.' She prattled away easily to Alistair, while Josh's mind went on a voyage of its own.

He recalled how Yang had wanted to go to a four-day classical music festival in Eilat. Initially he suggested that she go by bus on her own, wary that if he went with her, they might be spotted together. On top of that, the music festival was taking place during Chanukah and he knew in his heart that he should be home with the family, but he was torn. As much as he wanted to be with his children and grandchildren, the thought of four heavenly days in Eilat with Yang had its own power of allure. In the end he found a compromise. He would drive down to Eilat with her for the music festival, drive back and then fly to England for the last four days of Chanukah. He did not want to chance staying in a hotel, so they would rent a holiday apartment and would attend the concerts separately.

The concerts took place in the auditorium of the Royal Beach Hotel. When he arrived, the reception area was abuzz with chatter and anticipation. Brochures were distributed, cocktails offered and canapés provided in abundance.

Just as Josh was about to devour a mini profiterole, someone slapped him on the back and greeted him exuberantly.

'Are you here with your colleagues, spending all the money you earn from me?' Josh recognized him immediately as one of their wealthiest clients. 'I just noticed that rather delicious looking Chinese girl from your office, so I thought perhaps you were all here on a work outing.'

'*Yang*, is she here?' Josh replied in fake wonder.

'Yes didn't you know? Don't you converse in your office? You know what they say about all work and no play. She looked a little forlorn so I might offer to take her for a drink after the concert.' Josh was in total despair, but was helpless to prevent it. He had little choice but to return to the apartment afterwards and wait for her to come back. He was sure she would accept the invitation, as she wouldn't want to spurn one of their most influential clients.

He remembered his anguish when he pictured her laughing and drinking with him. Why should she prefer to be with Josh when she could be with someone young, handsome and extremely wealthy? In comparison, what did Josh have to offer, other than a relationship hidden away under a cloak of concealment? When Yang returned, she had reassured him that he was the only man she loved. It didn't help however, when she went off with the client for a nightcap on each of the subsequent evenings.

Rica stood up to take her leave, prompting Josh to emerge from his stupor. 'Hope we meet again soon. Can't wait for my Haagen Daz!'

The two weary travellers made their way to their hotel after an uneventful journey back to Beijing. Josh called the Investigation Agency to tell Mr. Wong that he had thought it over, and perhaps Yang might have studied piano after all.

'Ok I follow up that lead. Please call me again tomorrow morning.'

Chapter Eleven

"If I am not for myself, who will be for me?
If I am only for myself, what am I?
If not now, when?"
Hillel the Elder

Thursday 7th November 2019. Beijing

When Josh called the second time, Mr Wong informed him apologetically 'sorry no more sighting of Yang, but' he added triumphantly 'bank gives information. Yang's father open Chinese restaurant in Belize. '*Belize'* Josh repeated in disbelief.

'Remember, you told me Yang had Belize passport, her father work there. You said she thought passport from there help her get into English university because Belize was British Honduras. I not find more information on Yang. Sorry.'

Josh thanked the investigator for all his efforts and went to find Alistair. 'I do believe we have come to the end of our adventures' Josh informed him regretfully, repeating his conversation with Mr. Wong.

Alistair was unusually quiet and thoughtful for a few minutes before consulting his phone. He showed Josh the map of the Caribbean on the screen.

'I've never been to Belize, but I am told it is a magnificent country to visit. I was actually planning a trip to the Caribbean myself early next year. I've some investments in a Cayman Island bank and over the years have built up a friendship with my financial advisor there, who keeps trying to persuade me to visit. It would be my pleasure and privilege to continue our excursions and accompany you to Belize, before I go on to the Cayman Islands. I don't suppose it should be too difficult to locate Yang's father. How many Chinese restaurants can there be in Belize?'

Although Josh knew it was not a feasible option to fly halfway round the globe in search of a Chinese restaurant, he decided to let Alistair down gently, by promising him he would think about it. While Alistair had meetings that morning, Josh spent time at a shopping outlet in preparation for his return home. As he stressed to Alistair 'nineteen grandchildren will be expecting a gift from China.'

He returned to his room to pack his belongings but as he did so, the words of a song kept rewinding in his mind. It was a very popular Hebrew melody called "I Have Not Loved Enough" composed by Naomi Shemer, considered to be the First Lady of Israeli song and poetry. The words reflected on all the things still left to do in life and the line *'If not now when'* taken from a well-known rabbinical saying kept repeating itself over and over and would simply not leave him. His trip to Shanghai, which had started as a brief incursion into lunacy, had developed into an adventure of mammoth proportions.

Josh thought about his life. He considered himself a good person. Apart from his liaison with Yang he had basically tried to live up to the expectations others had of him. First his parents, then his wife and as each new addition to the family came along, his children and grandchildren. He never wanted to hurt them. In his mind, he managed to separate that life from the life he led during his 'enriched years' in Israel, as he liked to think of them. When those days ended, he had returned to his life in Hendon, conforming to everything expected by his wife, children and community. He now recognised that this was the first time in years that he was actually invigorated. He was thoroughly enjoying the holiday, savouring every moment. With Miriam, their annual holiday usually constituted a trip with their friends from the community to a country retreat. When not fervently praying, they engaged in serious debates and attended talks by esteemed religious figures.

This was the way of life that Miriam loved. She was deeply spiritual and always felt connected to a higher power, which gave her a clear sense of purpose and motivated every aspect of her life. Finding great beauty in every facet of the religion, she welcomed Shabbat as the day when she could step away from her busy week and immerse herself in contemplation, learning and prayer. Adherence to the ancient laws of the Torah in every possible way gave Miriam fulfilment, clarity and connection. In her opinion anyone who could not share those feelings was missing out on one of the greatest gifts the Jewish people had been given. Miriam did not see the restrictions as deprivations. Quite the contrary, they gave order and substance to her life.

She was a good mother and had instilled her deep convictions in all the children. Josh often wished he could share her sincere and strong beliefs. Outwardly he tried to play the part, but inwardly he knew it was all an act, one at which he had become adept. Appraising his life, he realised that the years were slipping by. This might be his last chance to seize the moment and do something purely for himself.

Why not travel to Belize with Alistair? All he had to do was call Miriam and tell her that the contract could only be completed in Belize, again just another distortion of the truth. Miriam was no longer the sweet freckle-faced girl he had first met. Now, in her advancing years, she was even more constrained by her rigidity. Unworldly, she would never think to doubt his word. In fact, most probably she had never heard of Belize and would certainly have no idea where it was. Was he insane he asked himself, struck by the absurdity of the whole idea? It was just a daydream, one of Alistair's hare-brained schemes. Of course he wouldn't go.

He went in search of Alistair, to inform him of his decision. He found him sitting in the lobby reading a

Chinese newspaper. As Josh approached, he saw that there were tears in Alistair's eyes.

'Do you remember me telling you about the French model who committed suicide in our hotel in Shanghai? It wasn't suicide after all. Apparently, her boyfriend, a famous French film star, murdered her. Her family came over from France straight away and were adamant that no way would she have taken her own life. Her career was just taking off and she had spoken to her parents the night before, telling them excitedly about her new job. They insisted that an investigation be launched and shortly afterwards the boyfriend confessed. He could no longer live with himself in the knowledge of his horrendous crime, committed in a moment of unbearable jealousy. She told him she had fallen in love with someone else and he killed her in a frenzied rage.'

Although Josh couldn't read the Chinese newspaper, he picked it up to look at the photograph of the couple, both looking glamorous and loving. With a start, Josh uttered 'I recognize him. Where would I know him from?' Instantly, his mind went back to the scene when he had emerged from his bedroom at the Waldorf Astoria Hotel and almost bumped into a good-looking young man, who plainly wanted to avoid conversation with him.

'No wonder he wouldn't talk to me, he didn't want to be identified.'

Inspired, Alistair interjected 'Perhaps that explains why we were followed and you were pushed. He was trying to eliminate you as a witness.' A vision, which had been lurking in the dark recesses of his memory suddenly came back to Josh, as a flash of that handsome but haunted face stared down at him on Nanjing Road in Shanghai.

'It also explains why there seemed to be a lot of activity going on in the bedroom next door,' Josh commented, 'which at the time didn't strike me as strange.' As they continued to discuss the case, Josh asked Alistair if he thought it was his moral duty to go to the police.

'If her boyfriend had not made a full confession then I would agree that you should, but he has, so I really don't think you can add very much, other than to claim that he possibly tried to kill you, twice. If you did go forward, you could well be detained in China as a witness. On balance, I would advise you, my lawyer friend, to keep this information to yourself.'

Although such a dastardly crime as murder could never be condoned, Josh was shocked to recognise that jealousy could propel someone to such horrific lengths. He shuddered at the thought that someone normally level-headed could be driven to behave so grotesquely. One read in the newspaper all the time about gruesome murders. Invariably the neighbours described the murderer as "just a regular sweet guy, you know the sort to call in to look after the children if you needed to pop out". This was a standard clichéd feature of reporting, but it raised a shocking thought in Josh's mind. If we are incapable of recognizing such tendencies in others, do we know what we could potentially do ourselves? Where did the drive to kill come from? Were the fervours and furies motivating such a dreadful deed and rendering it compelling, buried deep inside us all?

With such morbid thoughts suffusing his mind, a deep feeling of sadness engulfed him, intensified by the knowledge that this would be the end of their travels. The words *'if not now then when"* floated back into his head. Without giving himself an opportunity to retract, he exclaimed 'So how do we get to Belize?'

Alistair could hardly contain his joy. Immediately, he went online to check flights before Josh could change his mind. They discussed their various travel options which were limited, since direct flights between Asia and Latin America were sparse. 'The trip will necessitate a stopover in Canada or America.'

'Anything to Calgary' Josh inquired hopefully?' I've a cousin living there and it would be wonderful to visit him. As well as being cousins, despite the distance, we have also been friends since childhood and I know he has had a number of medical problems recently.'

'As it happens there is one out to Calgary this evening, should I book it?'

'YES!' Josh blurted, shocked by his own unexpected spontaneity. 'I'll email my cousin, asking if we can stay with them over Shabbat.'

'As much as I enjoy spending your Shabbat with you, there are a number of auction houses I want to visit, so I'll book a hotel. Last time I was there I saw a couple of stuffed dogs for auction. Guess what they would have fetched if they were in good condition?'

'No idea, what would they have fetched?'

'A ball' joked Alistair.

They had both visited Calgary on previous occasions so agreed that they would only spend a short time there before continuing to Belize.

Chapter Twelve

"Strive not to be a success,
but rather to be of value."
Albert Einstein

Friday 8th November 2019. Calgary

Settled in their seats for the first leg of the long haul to Canada, Josh asked Alistair a question that had piqued his curiosity since they first met. 'Have you ever been in love?'
'Well Josh, you have been blatantly honest with me about your love life, so I'm going to reveal to you my spectacularly embarrassing fiasco in the realms of passion and romance.

We need to go back to 1977, when I was twenty one years old. My study partner for one of my courses at Cambridge was a pretty, vivacious young girl from Edinburgh aptly named Bonnie. We spent a lot of time together and then one day, quite unexpectedly she told me she was in love with me. I was flattered and happily entered into a new chapter of my life, with a girlfriend. Her father was a parish vicar and her mother a schoolteacher, so our innocent kisses and hand holding were quite compatible with her strict upbringing. She told me quite simply that she was a virgin and would wait until we were married. I had not actually proposed or told her I loved her, but I just fell in with her plans. I didn't have any sensual feelings for her, but just presumed that it would gradually happen.

When it came to Christmas, she invited me to spend the holiday season with her family in Edinburgh. They were all warm and welcoming. I could see that her young sister Kylie worshipped Bonnie and she followed us around constantly. Bonnie asked me if we could announce our engagement to her family. We agreed that we would tell them as soon as her older brother Angus arrived on Christmas Day. When he walked in I was immediately captivated by his beauty and in that instant all the feelings I should have had for Bonnie, were transferred to him. Like a thunderbolt, the shocking realisation hit me that I must be gay or as it was known back in those days homosexual or queer. Naturally I kept it to myself and went ahead with our engagement. I was still in denial because it was most certainly not the way of life I had visualised for myself, yet every time I was near Angus I was overwhelmed by the desire to caress him, an arousal that I simply never experienced with Bonnie.

On New Year's Eve I went into the kitchen with Angus to pour the champagne. He had been so friendly to me all week and somehow I sensed vibes telling me he shared my feelings. I looked up and saw that we were standing under the mistletoe. Without thinking, I took him in my arms, told him that I was in love with him and kissed him on the lips. With a horrified expression he immediately pushed me away shouting "you are disgusting."

Bonnie and Kylie chose that moment to come into the kitchen, witnessing the whole humiliating scene and their hysterical screaming brought their parents in. It was the worst moment of my life.

Early the next morning I called a taxi and waited on a freezing platform at the station, until the first train arrived. Returning to Cambridge, Bonnie changed her course, and needless to say, we were both equally keen to avoid each other.

Have you ever done or said anything that you have lived to regret?' he asked, turning to Josh.

'Well to quote my beloved Winston, "*In the course of my life I have often had to eat my words, and I must confess that I have always found it a wholesome diet!*"

'I assume you have learnt all his quotes? 'Alistair asked jokingly.

'Not quite, but I do like his epitaph *"I am ready to meet my Maker. Whether my Maker is prepared for the ordeal of meeting me is another matter."* Sorry, please continue with your story Alistair.'

'After that mortifying debacle I was extremely cautious, but I did find someone else. I had bought a home in Rome and Stefan was the architect who designed the renovations. Like you and Yang, we also shared five glorious years together until he became sick. We had never heard of AIDS then, so it came as a devastating shock to be told that he was dying from it.

I had a friend from my Cambridge days who specialized in infectious diseases at the Middlesex Hospital, so I arranged for Stefan to be transferred there from the hospital in Rome. The Middlesex had a ward exclusively for AIDS patients and he received the very best care. He died twelve months after being diagnosed. I was left utterly heartbroken and despondent, but knew that I was the lucky one. I was alive and fortunately had not contracted the virus. I threw myself into cataloguing my snuff bottles, a therapeutic distraction to alleviate my grief.

One particular day in April 1987 is forever imprinted on my memory. Princess Diana came to officially open the unit. Stefan was sitting in a chair when she came into his room, illuminating it with her stunning beauty. There were no photographers with her, so her obvious warmth was not for the benefit of the camera. She held his hand and sat chatting for ten minutes, enabling him to give voice to his plight. At that time, public sympathy did not match the private pain suffered by AIDS patients, so Diana's small gesture had a tremendous impact on him. Ultimately, I think she did more than anyone else to remove the stigma surrounding the virus.

Like the rest of the world, I was horrified when her life ended in such a tragic way in 1997. Although most people knew of her philanthropy and benevolence from the press, I had witnessed her sweetness and sensitivity first hand. I was in London at the time and I've never seen such outpourings of grief. I walked past Kensington Palace a few days later to see the floral tributes and the memory of the fragrance still lingers with me to this day.

I have another delightful anecdote about Diana,' Alistair continued. 'Did you ever watch that satirical TV puppet show, "*Spitting Image?*" Caricatures of politicians and the Royal Family were lampooned outrageously.'

'One of my favourites,' Josh responded. 'Unfortunately, television was a complete taboo in our house, but I used to slip out and watch it with a friend. We would try to enjoy a decadent takeaway, whilst choking with laughter at the absurd humour.'

'Well, Stephen Fry, whom I know from my days in Footlights, tells an amusing story about that program. It was New Year's Day and Charles and Diana called on Stephen for tea. As they were leaving with their entourage, she whispered in Stephen's ear "I must be home in time to watch Spitting Image. ***They*** hate it ***of course,*** but I absolutely adore it." I wonder what your friend Winnie would have said about his distant cousin Diana.'

'He might have said "*It is not in our power to anticipate our destiny*" 'which in her case would have been fortunate.' Josh replied.

'So you see,' Alistair continued, 'I well understand illicit partnerships which have to be kept secret. There was never any option at that time of coming out, my parents would have been horrified. Since then, my snuff bottles have become my passion and constant companion. As MY great literary hero once said "*One's real life is so often the life that one does not lead.*"

You like to quote from your hero; I thought I would quote from mine.' Josh raised a questioning eyebrow in curiosity.

'Isn't it obvious?' Alistair countered, encouraging Josh to guess. He thought of Confucius, Hemingway and Mark Twain then it hit him. Of course, the authorial giant who Alistair was quoting was also the theatrical character he conjured up in Josh's mind with his eloquence, wit and whimsically insightful stories. He was even one of Churchill's favourites.

'Oscar Wilde!'

'Yes exactly, Oscar Fingal O'Flahertie Wills Wilde. I still feel intense personal pain when I think about the undeserved cruelty he suffered. In De Profundis he wrote "*The gods are strange. It is not our vices only they make instruments to scourge us. They bring us to ruin through what in us is good, gentle, humane, loving*".

As you might guess I can go on for hours about him. His fund of knowledge was inexhaustible. What he didn't know, he simply invented. On one occasion at a dinner table, he was taken up on his boast that he could talk on any subject, immediately and spontaneously. One lady suggested The Queen. Without hesitation he countered "*The Queen is not a subject.*"

Josh thought back over his many conversations with Alistair, aware that it was sometimes difficult to discern whether it was Alistair’s or Oscar’s words, as they seemed to skilfully intertwine.

Josh seized a pause in Alistair's flow to relate his own anecdote. 'Apparently, on one occasion Churchill was asked to choose an icon from history to invite for drinks and dinner. No doubt the anticipated response was a great warier, like Wellington or Julius Caesar, but no, he replied Oscar Wilde.'

'I can't think of any two people with more to recommend them as dinner companions and they were both masters of the one line insulting game.'

'Yes,' Josh agreed. 'My favourite was Churchill's famous comment to Lady Astor when she rebuked him for being drunk.'

Mimicking Churchill's distinctive voice Alistair continued. "And you madam are ugly. But I shall be sober in the morning."

Resuming his tale of amorous encounters, Alistair continued. 'My only other romantic dalliance was with Ernest, who led a rather outlandish lifestyle. A beguiling Oxford graduate who lectured in English literature, we met through our mutual love of Oscar. He had even renamed himself after the main character in “The Importance of being Earnest.” He used to host “Wilde" themed dinner parties, where we would all dress up in the sort of clothes Oscar would have worn and converse only in Oscar speak, as we designated it. Oscar would have loved the adulation and admiration we bestowed upon him, but despite all our jocularity we always paid homage to his tragic downfall. He bore the many indignities which were heaped upon him with fortitude and without displaying malice or ill feeling. Sorry, I digress.

Fortunately, Ernest made his feelings for me very clear, as I had no intentions of making the same blunder twice, and he invited me to move into his house. I had my own home, so I agreed to stay for part of the week. His was a large, rambling old house and I could come and go as I pleased.

I arrived at Ernest's house one day but there was no sign of him, so I started looking around to see if he was in the garden. Two doors next to each other were at the back of the kitchen. One opened on to the garden and the other was always locked. By mistake, I tried the locked door and unexpectedly it opened. Naturally, my insatiable curiosity was ignited and led me down a staircase and through a tunnel. At the end of the tunnel a second door led up more stairs into another house.

Warily, I walked through the kitchen into the living room, where to my initial embarrassment I encountered a rather tall lady with long blonde hair, pirouetting in the centre. Bedecked in a sequined dress, high heels and an excess of tasteless flashy jewellery, she was twirling about in front of a full-length mirror, This *lady,* to my initial confusion, spoke with Ernest's unmistakable voice saying 'Hi, Alistair, you have uncovered my little secret, but no matter. I was waiting for the right moment to introduce you to Gwendolen, my alter ego.

Without the slightest embarrassment, he then proceeded to show me his array of outrageous clothes scattered around the house. He told me that whenever he went out of the front door of his second house, he became Gwendolen, the heroine from The Importance of Being Earnest. He was sure that no one who knew Ernest, the University Professor, would identify him with the strange lady living in the house beyond.

Now I know this will sound hypocritical to you, but his dubious lifestyle did not sit well with my own values, and I gradually distanced myself from Ernest's life.'

'On the contrary Alistair, knowing you as I now do, I don't think you were a hypocrite.'

They were both totally exhausted by the time they touched down in Calgary after the ten hour flight. Josh's cousin and wife Sylvia were eagerly awaiting him at the airport and looking forward to hosting him over Shabbat.

Once supper was over Josh excused himself as intense tiredness overcame him. When he finally awoke he was shocked to see it was lunchtime and Joshua had already returned from morning prayers at the synagogue.

Chapter Thirteen

"Better to remain silent and be thought a fool than to speak and remove all doubt"
Abraham Lincoln

Saturday 9th November 2019. Calgary

Josh was very fond of his cousin also called Joshua. Their mothers, Freda and Beatrice were sisters who had come to Britain on the Kindertransport. They had both named their sons after their late father, who had been murdered in Auschwitz.

Josh's mother Freda had married and stayed in England. Beatrice had married a Canadian and moved to Calgary, where Joshua and his sister had grown up.

Despite the fact that International travel was not so prevalent at that time, Joshua's father recognized the importance for the sisters to see each other as frequently as possible. Fortunately, he was able to afford the luxury of a family trip to the UK every summer, which not only gave the sisters an opportunity to be together, but also gave Josh and Joshua a chance to forge a lifelong friendship. Originally based on cousinly rivalry, it matured into a deep mutual admiration.

Despite Josh's close relationship with his cousin and his implicit trust in him, he could not divulge the secret of his affair with Yang and the true reason for his travels. He hated to lie to him, but knew it was unfair to burden his cousin with such a weighty secret, considering how well Joshua knew his family.

After lunch Joshua suggested a walk to the nearby Heritage Park, a popular tourist destination, but Josh was content to relax in the armchair and reflect on their many shared memories. Sylvia tactfully left them alone to enjoy their reminiscing.

'Do you remember how shocked we were on that holiday in Wales?' Josh reflected.

The journey, when they were both fourteen, had been of profound significance to Josh. They had piled into a camper van with their parents to drive north and explore the picturesque Welsh countryside. At their age, his three older sisters were only too happy to be left at home in London, with their female Canadian cousin.

The two boys had been unaware when they set out, but the trip was intended to be a bittersweet voyage into the past for their mothers. They were going to visit Gwrych Castle, which had been home to some three hundred young Jewish refugees including Freda and Beatrice, for the duration of the war. They had managed to flee the Nazis in the months before World War Two, coming to Britain on the Kindertransport.

Whilst traveling in the camper van the sisters revealed their traumatic shared history, which came as a total shock to Josh. They spoke of the day in December 1938, when they were standing on the platform in Berlin, shivering from cold and fear, saying goodbye to their parents, amidst a scene of devastating sadness. Freda aged sixteen and Beatrice at fourteen, were amongst the older children and tried to be stoic. They were encouraged to help with the younger children, who could not understand what was happening and were crying hysterically. The older girls tried to comfort them by holding their hands and telling them they were going on an adventure. Freda remembered how their mother had run alongside the train as it pulled away shouting a brave farewell. 'Goodbye girls, just look forward, don't look back.'

After a long arduous journey by train and boat they arrived at Liverpool Street Station, where the children were met and dispersed throughout the country. At first, the two sisters were horrified when they arrived at Gwrych Castle, once a magnificent edifice, now cold and derelict. Nothing worked. There was no heating, no lighting or plumbing and they had to sleep on straw on the stone floor. The children realised that they all needed to help make it fit for habitation. Once settled in, they understood that they were some of the lucky ones. News filtered through about other children who had been placed with foster families not overly sympathetic to their plight, without the comfort of a sibling and without even a common language.

After the visit to the castle, the sisters lifted the gloom by talking of lasting friendships forged during those years and relating funny incidents. Beatrice told them the tale of the hideous monster which had given her nightmares when they first arrived. One of the boys had pointed out an apparition moving about in the field below the castle, convincing the girls that it was a grotesque headless creature. It was months before the poor girls realised that it was nothing more than a black and white sheep that appeared headless due to its black head merging into the shadows of the hedge. Finding great amusement in the story and not wanting to dwell on the sadness, Josh and Joshua spent the rest of the holiday making up ghost stories to frighten each other.

'I had no idea before then that our mums had four siblings who did not survive.' Josh ruminated, 'did your mum ever talk about them?'

'No, never.' Joshua confirmed. 'I knew that our grandparents had all died in the Holocaust but it was a taboo subject so I didn't ask, even though I was curious to learn more about it.'

'Same with us,' Josh agreed. 'Before that holiday I had no idea about their siblings or their Kindertransport experiences. Sending their children away in a desperate effort to save them must have been the hardest test of love to befall a parent.'

To lift the melancholy mood, Josh reminded Joshua of their visit to the nearby beach at Colwyn Bay.

'Do you remember how cold it was?'

'Yes, we sat in deck chairs huddled under blankets, shivering incessantly, just so we could say we had been to the beach.'

The cousins spent the rest of the afternoon in easy compatibility, regaling each other with anecdotes from their past. They were both amazed when Sylvia came in to inform them it was already time for Havdalah, the ceremony to mark the end of Shabbat.

Joshua removed the Havdalah set from the glass cabinet. A small embossed silver parrot with a removable head contained the fragrant spices. Josh admired the unusual spice box.

'It's exquisite; I've never seen one like that before.'

'Yes,' Joshua agreed, 'in fact just before mum passed away she told me the story behind it. When they left Germany they were allowed to take one small case each, but no valuables. Unbeknown to his girls, our grandfather had hidden this spice box inside a slipper in your mum's suitcase. Your mum, being the older sister, was always very protective towards my mum, little Trixie, as she always called her. When she discovered this piece, she thought it would make her little sister sad to see a reminder from home, so she didn't show her. On my parents' wedding day, your mum presented it to my mum as a gift from their father. Mum treasured it lovingly throughout her life, but also felt pangs of guilt. She knew that Aunt Freda had given away not only her one link with her parents, but also one of her favourite pieces from their home. I think Mum would be very pleased if you were to take it back to England and become the custodian of this family heirloom.'

Josh was visibly moved by the warm-hearted gesture, but reluctant to accept.

'You must take it' Sylvia insisted. 'He was planning to defy doctors' orders and bring it to you in London.'

'In that case, thank you. I'll gratefully accept and think of Aunt Trixie every time we use it.'

Amidst scenes of emotional farewells at the airport, the cousins parted company.

Chapter Fourteen

"Believe you can and you're halfway there."
Theodore Roosevelt

Sunday 10th November 2019. San Pedro Ambergris Caye

On the second leg of their trip from Calgary to Belize, Josh couldn't wait to show Alistair his acquisition. Alistair immediately took out his professional magnifying glass in order to appraise it.

'This is just magnificent and quite old,' he murmured. 'If you look closely at the legs you can see a German city silver hallmark. Since city hallmarks were abolished around 1880, this must have been made before that date. Even though German silver is actually made up of copper, nickel and zinc, this piece is extremely valuable because of its age, rarity and craftsmanship.'

'Needless to say,' Josh responded, 'it is the sentimental value that is important to me, but as always, your vast knowledge never fails to amaze me!'

Alistair was in a talkative mood. He was a natural performer and Josh had come to look forward to the sagas which flowed with such verve and ease, as he embellished them and brought everything so vividly to life. Alistair was also exuberant over his latest acquisition, which prompted him to explain the intricacies of its painting.

'The artist would take a small bamboo paintbrush with a curved end and using pigments, would carefully manipulate the brush into the narrow head of the bottle in order to paint on the inside, creating perfect scenic artwork. Invariably, these scenes imitated art emanating originally from famous Chinese tales, which often told the story of the wealth and power of the last Imperial Dynasty. The bottle in the front of my book was the one that my father bought me when I was ten, illustrating the cutest Shih Tzu dog. This sparked my lifelong fascination with snuff bottles and Shih Tzu dogs. I take it with me to remind me of Chino, my dog back home.'

'Who looks after Chino when you are traveling?'

'Housekeepers look after him, as well as my two parrots, although I am tempted to sack them for teaching the parrots to sing in unison "I feel pretty and witty and gay" all the time.' Alistair paused for breath giving Josh the opportunity to speak.

'Did you buy the dog in Italy?'

'No I bought him in England. It's a long story but I think we have time,' he added.

'James, a friend of mine since our days at Rugby, trained as a vet, then built up a reputation as a successful dog whisperer. I told him I wanted to buy a Shih Tzu dog. He suggested I come over to stay with them in England and accompany him to the Crufts dog show, where his dog would be competing in the obedience section. That way I would be able to see all the various breeds of dog, in case I decided on a different variety. He offered to help me find a reliable breeder, which he pointed out was essential before choosing a dog. Firstly choose a trustworthy well-established breeder and check out his credentials before choosing the dog!'

'I had no idea that choosing a dog was such a complicated procedure,' Josh commented.

'If you are looking for a top class pedigree dog it certainly is, and the cost of such dogs can be surprisingly high. I came over to stay with James and his wife Felicity, who had been kind hosts to me on many occasions. Their daughter Clare is now a qualified vet herself, but when I first started to visit, she was just a young girl, and she always wanted me to read her a bedside story. I started reading "The Canterville Ghost" to her, one of Oscar's best in my opinion. Have you read it?'

'Probably, a long time ago,' Josh replied, 'remind me.'

'It is a humorous short story about an American family who move into a haunted English country house. They had been warned not to buy it, since it was haunted by Sir Simon De Canterville. He was a nobleman who had killed his wife, and after his own death was trapped in the house as its resident ghost. Far from frightening the family, they turned the tables and devised their own methods to torment him. Clare loved the story and when it was time for her to go to bed she would say "Uncle Ally stairs," which was her little joke to ask me to come upstairs to continue the story. Anyway I am getting side-tracked. I just loved the Crufts show, and even if I hadn't decided on a Shih Tzu, I would have fallen in love with one.'

'What made you so sure Shih Tzu was the breed you wanted?'

'As well as being the cutest shaggy hound I've ever seen with a long silky coat flowing to the ground, it also happens to have deep roots in Chinese history, being the favourite pet dog of royal Chinese families during the Ming dynasty. On the reverse side of my snuff bottle a story is told in Chinese characters about the Empress of China, Tzu Hsi. She issued an edict that anyone caught torturing palace dogs would be put to death. During her reign, the Dalai Lama of the time presented her with a pair of Shih Tzus. It is said that they had their own palace and were trained to sit up and wave their front paws whenever she visited.'

Following Crufts, James took me to a DogFest, which is a festival of fun for dogs and their owners. There were many different programs and competitions, but the celebrity look-alike contest was priceless. Each canine contestant stood next to a photograph of his human doppelgänger. I imagine that some of the photos had been altered and features exaggerated for comical effect, but the results were absurdly funny.

James then helped me to locate a top breeder, whose prize-winning dog had recently given birth to a large litter. He graciously offered me the first choice and I chose the most inquisitive and outgoing puppy. I returned to Italy and James looked after Chino, as I named him, for a few weeks until he was old enough to travel. I came back to London and we then made our way back to Italy by Eurostar in a camper van, but that's another story' he added as he saw Josh fighting to stay awake.

Landing in Belize, they took a short domestic flight to San Pedro on Ambergris Caye. This was the largest of the many small islands. They had been told that the islands and the tourist areas of Belize City were safe, but had been warned that crime was rife in certain parts of the mainland. Belize, like the rest of Central America, was an ideal transit country for illegal drug shipments from Columbia to Mexico. The streets were plagued with hoodlums belonging to rival gangs, all vying for their share. The police tried to control the situation, but dealing with ruthless killers who had large quantities of guns and explosives, they were not always successful.

Refreshed, Josh and Alistair decided to explore the island, traveling in a golf buggy which seemed to be the primary mode of transport.

Since they were never far from the sparkling aqua coastline of the Caribbean Sea, they decided to dip their feet in the water and were pleasantly surprised at how warm it was. It brought back fond recollections of the times Josh had spent on the beaches in Israel.

Making full use of their golf buggy they drove round the island scouring it for Chinese restaurants, while at the same time savouring the tropical ambience. Having exhausted every possibility on Ambergris Caye, they succumbed to the tempting aromas emanating from the last stop and decided to sample the cuisine.

Scrutinizing the menu, they both managed to find an option which sounded suitable, but when Josh tried to explain that he wanted his dish without meat, the waiter vanished as hastily as he had appeared.

'Do you think I offended him?' At that moment the waiter reappeared together with the Chinese chef. Alistair clarified that his friend wanted his meal without any meat or chicken included. The chef nodded eagerly, adding that he presumed the chicken broth in which it was cooked would not pose a problem. When Alistair further elaborated the situation, the chef beamed and nodded with comprehension.

'Ahhh kosher yes? I work on cruise ship, I know about kosher. I cook you fish in silver foil.'

Since the chef seemed so helpful, it occurred to Josh to ask if by chance he knew Yang's father. The name didn't mean anything to him, but he told Josh that the majority of Chinese lived in Belize City, where there was a Belize Chinese Association which might be able to help locate him.

They thanked the chef for his help, and he went off to prepare their meals.

'Should we go to Belize City tomorrow?' Alistair asked. Josh had mixed feelings.

Although he wanted to find Yang's father, would that bring him any closer to finding Yang, and did he really want to find her? He wanted to know that she was safe, but selfishly, not that she had found happiness with someone else. He was enjoying his holiday and he didn't want to spoil it yet, by discovering where life had taken Yang without him.

'Let's book that rainforest trip that you found for tomorrow. I know you are looking forward to it and especially to seeing the howler monkeys.' Alistair had mentioned to Josh how he had been enamoured by the idea of these monkeys famous for their loud howl.

Chapter Fifteen

"Conversation about the weather
is the last refuge of the unimaginative."
Oscar Wilde

Monday 11th November 2019. Belize City

The next morning Alistair and Josh took the ferry from San Pedro to Belize City and a taxi to the entrance of the rainforest. The expert guide took them through the undergrowth, explaining the medicinal properties of herbs, barks and plants. As they were led deeper into the area, they viewed stunning lush green mounds, natural springs, coconut trees and a profusion of different wildlife. As they passed ancient Mayan ruins, burial sites and altars, the guide broke his running commentary to exclaim indignantly.

'Can you imagine that in 2013 a construction company destroyed one of Belize's largest Mayan pyramids with bulldozers, simply to extract crushed rock for a new road project. It was one of the most important sites in Northern Belize and dated back two thousand three hundred years.'

Cries of horrified disbelief came from the group, as the guide continued.

'It wasn't even a mistake, they were well aware that it was an ancient structure, but they wanted road fill and were simply too lazy to excavate from a quarry.'

Before they could discuss the subject further, they heard a noise resembling a loud air raid siren. Alistair and Josh were fascinated as they watched the appropriately-named Howler monkeys, swinging from tree to tree in their natural habitat. As soon as one monkey started howling, others joined in to make a hideous cacophony of sounds.

On the ferry back to San Pedro, the motion of the boat sent Josh into a daydream. He imagined himself taking on a new identity and living out the rest of his life in this idyllic distant corner of the world. Although he knew it was just a mad fantasy, he thought about those people who had engineered their own disappearance. He recalled an article he had read, about a man who had gone out one morning to buy cigarettes from the corner shop and never returned, leaving his wife and two small children to face all the debts he had accumulated. Twenty three years later he was discovered living in a remote location, having taken on the identity of a man who had died years earlier. Only when the dead man's son started researching his genealogy was his deception uncovered.

Even in his most fanciful daydreams, Josh could never imagine disappearing completely from his family life. He knew his children would move heaven and earth to find him, although he did have his doubts about Miriam. Almost like ships passing in the night, they exchanged banal comments when their paths crossed in the hallway at home. Both seemed to be on their own private journey, hers spiritual, his more pragmatic, as he headed from his study to the kitchen. Sometimes in his mind, he replaced Miriam with Yang and luxuriated in contemplation of marital harmony, where they inhabited the house in a life of unfettered love and romance. Yet, his reveries never extend beyond the bounds of reason. His children and grandchildren would simply appear, adoration etched on their smiling faces as they gazed up at him. Surely that ***was*** his fulfilment in life, he told himself in frustrated and anguished self-admonishment.

Arriving in San Pedro he shook off his disturbing thoughts, quite horrified with himself for allowing ludicrous notions of disappearance to enter his mind. What was he thinking, he reprimanded himself. He constantly received text messages from the older grandchildren, asking when he was coming home. Although not allowed phones with access to the internet, approval was given for communication purposes only.

Their plan to explore Belize City the next day prompted them to book a luxury hotel there for the next evening, rather than returning to San Pedro. They were told that it would be perfectly safe, just as long as they didn't stray to the gangland areas.

Chapter Sixteen

"If a man is called to be a street sweeper, he should sweep streets even as a Michelangelo painted, or Beethoven composed music or Shakespeare wrote poetry. He should sweep streets so well that all the hosts of heaven and earth will pause to say,
'Here lived a great street sweeper who did his job well."
Martin Luther King Jr.

Tuesday 12th November 2019. Belize City

Josh had tried calling the Belize Chinese Association on a couple of occasions, in an attempt to locate Sammy's restaurant, but to no avail. Driving around Belize City on a tour bus the next morning, the two friends noticed the large number of Chinese who seemed to be living in Belize. They were also amused by the plethora of Chinese restaurants with telling names, like "Hop on the Won Ton" and "Wen do we eat".

'So much for me thinking there can't be many Chinese restaurants here.' Alistair quipped.'

A rotund, jolly lady called Bianca gave a running commentary on the bus. They were taken along narrow roads, the sparkling sea to one side, and many quaint colourful houses and assorted constructions scattered haphazardly on the other. Crossing the historic swing bridge, demarcating the north and south sides of Belize

City, Bianca described it as one of the few manually operated swing bridges in the world still in use, needing four strong men to move it. 'Fortunately', she added, 'it was only activated in times of emergency.'

The bus continued into a busier area with more shops and restaurants. Josh and Alistair agreed that for the sake of expediency, they should alight from the bus and embark on foot-soldiering. Wandering amiably along the narrow pavements, checking restaurants, stepping in and out of the road in order to avoid both cars and pedestrians, Alistair was in a jovial mood, regaling Josh with stories and childish jokes.

'Did you hear about the lawyer who sued an airline company after it lost his luggage? Sadly he lost his case!

Why is a doctor always calm? Because he has a lot of patients!'

'Did I ever mention that I have some medical training?' Josh interjected. 'I trained to do circumcisions.'

'You were a mohel?' Alistair asked incredulously.

Now it was Josh's turn to be surprised. 'You are acquainted with the word?'

'Who do you think circumcised me? It's not a practice totally restricted to Jewish babies you know. Anyway, when did you become a mohel?'

'Many years ago, it was during my most religious period. Just like the seven stages of man, I can define my own spiritual journey: acceptance, rebellion, righteousness, resignation, doubting, straying, and, he paused, 'not quite sure how to define this last one.'

'Was it a long training?'

'Yes there is a lot to learn and a lengthy apprenticeship.'

'So what prompted you?'

'Our son Matan was born with a serious blood infection. For the first two months, we didn't know if he would survive. Thankfully, he turned the corner and grew strong enough to have his circumcision, which we call the Brit. When the day came, our house overflowed with family, friends and neighbours spilling out into the garden. They had all helped during this difficult period, especially as Miriam was not functioning well. Joshua even came over from Canada especially for the occasion. A tremendous sense of anticipation filled the room. You could almost touch the heightened euphoria everyone was feeling.

I stood next to the mohel and he told the guests that the Brit is the father's responsibility to perform. Traditionally, he authorizes the mohel to carry it out on his behalf. However, unbeknown to anyone else, on this occasion I planned to do it myself.

A stunned silence filled the room when the mohel announced my intention, broken only by Miriam, who gave a horrified shriek from behind the screen where the women had gathered. To be honest it wasn't as dramatic as it sounds. The mohel had done all the preparations, so all I had to do was the final snip above the clamp. I can't tell you what an incredible feeling it gave me. At that moment I decided to become a mohel. Once I qualified, I would do one or two circumcisions a month, when it fitted in with my work.'

'So why did you stop?'

Josh's face clouded over.

'The main reason was because I was too busy at work but,' he hesitated, 'we have confided some of our most harrowing and traumatic times to each other and what I am about to reveal to you, is one of mine. On one occasion a baby died two days after I had performed his Brit. After an investigation I was totally exonerated, as the little boy had an undetected birth defect. Although innocent of blame, I was a completely tortured soul. I knew I could never live with myself if I should ever cause such a tragedy, so I decided to decline any further requests.

Deep in conversation, they had not noticed that the bustle of the shops had disappeared and they had strayed into a run-down area, with crumbling wooden houses behind broken corrugated fences, many riddled with bullet holes. A number of young men loitered on street corners.

'They don't look as friendly as most of the Belizeans we have met so far,' Alistair commented. 'How fast can you run?' Josh could hear his own heartbeat thumping in his chest. His running days were long past.

As they looked around, Josh felt a threatening undercurrent of danger. Out of the corner of his eye he could see one of the men sauntering towards them. Another two appeared from a different corner. Rigid with fear, there seemed little hope of escape when, out of nowhere a taxi thundered past honking its horn. The driver pulled up and gesticulated wildly for them to jump in. Despite having been cautioned to look for a green license plate denoting an official taxi driver, with no time to spare, they clambered in. Once they were in the back seat they heard the click, as the driver locked all the doors. Was that to protect them or so there was no escape? The driver turned to ask where he should take them. They were both still unnerved by their alarming experience, which was exacerbated by his menacing appearance, multiple scars criss-crossing his chilling features.

Remarkably though, his friendly demeanour belied this frightening vision. Grinning broadly he introduced himself as Mungo and then proceeded to admonish them for walking through the dangerous part of the city.

'I would never normally come over to this side of town, but I had to deliver some medicine. I was on my way back when I saw you in the mirror, so I turned the taxi round to pick you up. Did no-one warn you about walking around this neighbourhood? These guys have a very casual attitude towards violence. You could have been in mortal danger.'

Driving away from their potential assailants, Mungo appeared eager to talk about his life. He told them he had been born in the southern part of the city which was simply a lifelong battleground and very difficult to escape from.

'Drug trafficking is a multi-billion-dollar business in Belize and I used to be part of it. I was sucked into a life of violence and gangland murders, where members were paid in drugs and weapons. One day I woke up to my daughter sobbing hysterically in fear and I decided that I wanted a better life for my young family. Instead of prowling round the streets, I began to work long hard hours, in order to better the conditions we lived in. I even joined a project aimed at discouraging children from joining a gang, but with three thousand gang members roaming the streets day and night, it was not easy and my daughters lived in perpetual fear.

Despite English being the mother tongue of Belize, Mungo's thick Caribbean accent made it difficult to catch every word he said, but they understood enough of his story to be wary. Were they in the hands of a reformed gangster, or could they have simply been rescued from one danger, to face another.

They began to recognize a slightly more familiar side of town. Mungo slowed down then gradually cruised to a halt.

'Actually we are just passing my home and I need to give my daughter a lift, so I hope you don't object to me collecting her?'

Josh and Alistair gave each other warning looks, realising that they had little choice but to acquiesce. As they drew up outside his house, they became increasingly nervous. Would it be more perilous to wait for Mungo in the car, or to go inside and perhaps be subjected to other unforeseen perils? Their silent deliberations were settled, when he opened the car door for them, indicating that they should join him.

Following him into the house, they were taken aback by the sight that greeted them. Three pairs of big brown petrified eyes peered at them from behind a long, low, worn out sofa, where his daughters were all cowering.

'Don't worry girls these men won't hurt you' their father reassured them, as they emerged and threw their arms around him. Josh was greatly touched by the anomaly of this man's violent past and his obvious adoration for his children.

Leaving the house Mungo's youngest daughter accompanied them to the car. Her father suggested that Josh sit in the front seat, as his daughter was still too young. Reluctantly hoisting herself onto the seat next to Alistair, she cast terrified glances all around, yet within a minute she could be heard giggling at one of his silly jokes, then more laughter as he entertained her for the rest of the journey.

After their alarming experience, Josh and Alistair were content to return to the safety of their hotel and spend the rest of the evening relaxing, whilst discussing their day.

'How sad to be born into such violence,' Alistair commented, 'especially in contrast to the idyllic life so close by. Whilst we bask in the beauty of this splendid country, it's hard to imagine that violence and destruction are such a short distance away. I wish I could do something to help.'

'Altruistic words Alistair, but it would be a monumental task to improve the quality of their lives. Let's worry about more practical matters. I know we haven't exhausted all the Chinese eating establishments in Belize City yet, but would you fancy a trip to Belmopan tomorrow?'

'It should be interesting to visit,' Alistair agreed 'since it was built from scratch as the new capital, after hurricane Hattie destroyed most of the old Belize City. He then promptly disappeared, returning ten minutes later armed with a map of Belmopan.

'The concierge informs me that the best way to travel there is on the express bus, which goes along the quaintly-named Hummingbird Highway. According to him, it is one of the prettiest and most scenic routes in the country.

Chapter Seventeen

"All you need is love. But a little chocolate now and then doesn't hurt."
Charles M. Schulz

Wednesday 13th November 2019. Toledo District

Driving their golf buggy towards the bus terminal, to catch the Hummingbird Highway express, Alistair was startled by Josh's sudden exclamation to stop.

'Look over there.' He was pointing to a sign above a shop inscribed "*Belize Chocolate Boutique*".

'I hope you don't mind me mentioning it, but I've observed that you are a bit of a chocoholic.'

'Not at all' Alistair responded. 'You are absolutely correct, let's investigate.' Entering the shop they marvelled at the vast selection of mouth-watering items all made from chocolate, as well as the delectable fragrance. The owner was clearly delighted to find someone who shared his love of chocolate and happily showed them around, explaining the chocolate-making process from pod to final product.

'If you are interested, we organize day trips to the Toledo area of Belize where the pods grow, so that people can watch the process first hand.' Josh could sense the curiosity and interest in Alistair's response, when he asked how long the trip would take.

'The flight is about an hour. Actually, a group is just about to leave for the airfield.' Josh looked at Alistair, whose feelings were invariably written on his face.

'Well I don't know about you,' Josh announced with uncharacteristic spontaneity 'but I'll never be here again, so let's do it. We'll save Belmopan for another day.'

They arrived at the organic chocolate plant, where their guide took them through the whole process. The first stop was in the forest area where trees grew in profusion, with pods sprouting directly from the body of the tree. As he plucked one he spoke.

'When the pods start turning from green to yellow we pick them.' Carefully cutting round its middle and removing the top part of the hard shell, he offered the white goo-covered seeds for everyone to taste. They all agreed that it was surprisingly sweet.

'Now let's go to the greenhouse, where the beans are put in large wooden troughs to ferment for a few days before they are sun-dried then roasted.'

The processing plant was no less fascinating, where they saw the beans shelled before being crushed, to create cocoa nibs which were then ground to a soft paste.

'Since the paste in its raw form is 100% pure, it has a bitter taste, so at this stage we add butter, spices and flavours. Here is a spot of history before we finish. The Mayan people discovered the beans two thousand years ago and used them as currency. Three beans could be exchanged for one egg and one hundred for a live turkey.'

On their return flight Alistair told Josh that he had a confession to make. Interesting, Josh thought to himself, there must be something about our flights that prompts Alistair's confessions.

'You know you said that it's unlikely you will ever come here again, well I am quite smitten by everything, the people, the climate, not to mention the laid back lifestyle. SO……..' he paused, 'I am seriously considering buying a holiday home here.'

'Wow' Josh reacted. 'Wow again!' He was lost for words, as he tried to digest this information

Alistair continued, 'I've actually been in touch with an estate agent who is going to show me a condo on the appropriately-named Coco Beach just three kilometres from San Pedro. He told me that he used to live in New York where he and his wife both had high-powered jobs. They were earning a fortune, but were always too stressed to reap any benefit from their constantly-challenged lives. One day they simply decided to give it all up and come here to live. Now they lead an unrushed life, earning enough to live on, dabbling in real estate. They are able to savour the rest of the day relaxing, diving or exploring. No rush hour traffic to contend with or anxiety over crucial deadlines. No hysterical bosses expecting them to resolve fraught situations. Yes I know it sounds like a sales pitch, but his enthusiasm was infectious. Also, who knows, perhaps in some small way I can do something to help the plight of the street kids here.'

'Nice sentiments and intentions, but my advice would be not to get involved. It could be far too dangerous and you might easily put your life in jeopardy.'

'Yes I suppose you are right,' Alistair agreed.

'So, when are we going to see this property?' Josh asked, automatically including himself in the arrangements.

'No time like the present!'

The real estate agent was ebullient about the property, pointing out every feature in glowing terms. Despite knowing it was sales talk, it was hard to deny its magnificence. Indeed, the property was breath-taking and lived up to his description of barefoot luxury in paradise. Large windows in every room were open to views of white sandy beaches and palm trees at the edge of the glistening Caribbean Sea.

He pointed out that since Belize was an English speaking country all contracts and legal dealings would be in English.

'I suppose you guys are looking to retire here,' he added, doubtless assuming that they were a couple. Before Alistair took the opportunity for more theatricals, Josh quickly clarified.

'No no, I'm his legal advisor.' Josh could see that Alistair was displaying his eagerness for the place and aware of his spontaneous nature, sensed that it would do no harm to indicate his legal connections.

With promises to be in touch they returned to the hotel.

'I'm going to make an offer,' Alistair declared emphatically.

Chapter Eighteen

"Wise men speak because they have something to say; fools because they have to say something."
Plato

Thursday 14th November 2019. Belize City

Browsing through the fliers in the foyer of the hotel, Josh discovered that one of the most popular eating establishments in town was called "Yin and Yang". Deep down, Josh was sure that this must be ***The One.*** After all, it made total sense that Sammy would have named his restaurant after his beloved daughter. It had been abundantly clear during their stay in Israel, just how much Sammy idolized her. Now, reluctant to face the inevitable conclusion to his search, Josh was stalling. He even secreted the sheet when he saw Alistair approaching, trying to distract him with a suggestion.

'Since we were sublimely diverted yesterday, let's take our aborted trip to Belmopan today.' Admonishing him with mock exasperation Alistair responded.

'You think I'm unaware of your procrastinating tactics. I also read the pamphlet you just tried to conceal, advertising the best food in town! We are going there for lunch today.' Josh could spend hours deliberating over situations, whereas Alistair liked to live for the moment, often acting impulsively.

As soon as they walked in, Josh recognized Yang's father, and greeted him warmly.

'JOSH' Sammy said in astonishment, 'is it you, is it really you? I can't believe it,' he said with disbelief, 'what you doing here?'

Josh had decided that if he should find Sammy, it might be wiser not to mention his search for Yang. In his usual manner he camouflaged the truth by feigning incredulity at their supposedly chance meeting.

'I am here on business with my colleague Alistair, but we are also discovering the attractions of Belize.'

'Sit down, sit down, please be my guests.' He sat down with them and immediately began reminiscing about their time together in Israel. As he did so he had a troubled look on his face.

'You were very kind to us and to Yang, but I know we outstay our welcome. I always feel guilty and think I owe you detail.' Without giving Josh a chance to speak he continued.

'Liat and I live in very big house in best area of Shanghai, but we work there. I was chef and Liat housekeeper. The family are very rich and there is always cash and jewellery lying around. Each week we take little cash or sometimes jewellery and they never notice. I very ashamed but we do it to help Yang. One day, they catch us taking something and throw us out of house immediately.

They not call the police, but that is why we came to visit you and stay so long.

When we came back to China we found little home in Zhujiajiao, but then Liat had stroke and no longer talk. I decided to come to Belize to open Chinese restaurant. All my life this my big dream. I send back money to help look after Liat.' As he finished he looked relieved as if he had just been liberated from a heavy burden.

'I understand,' Josh told him sympathetically, 'and I am glad to see that your business is so successful.' Sammy smiled warmly.

'Yes and, you know, Yang is also very famous and successful.' Josh could feel his heart beating faster and faster.

'No! I haven't heard from her again since she left Tel Aviv.'

'Well she came back to visit us once in Zhujiajiao. She tell us she give up law and go to Beijing to learn piano at Music school. She had much success and moved to Rome. She sometimes play with important Rome Orchestra and she travel a lot. She is known as Yakira.' Alistair, who had been sitting quietly listening to their conversation, emitted an unexpected exclamation.

'Yakira! She is incredible; I've seen her perform a number of times in Rome.' All this was too remarkable and unbelievable for Josh who could hardly take it in.

'Yes I have brochure, I show you' Sammy said as he eagerly scuttled away. He returned with a program portraying Yang on the front cover sitting at a grand piano.

Josh could hardly breathe as he beheld her elfin beauty, enhanced by a new sleek hairstyle, short skirt and 5 inch heels. He read the synopsis of her career which hailed her as a dazzling and gifted pianist.

"Shakira is one of the most talented performers to hit the world stage in recent years, with spectacular stage presence and eye-catching outfits. No matter where she appears it is always to sell-out crowds, as she enthrals and captivates her audience with her pulsation of energy".

'Yang send me money to help Liat' Sammy continued, 'and she calls from time to time but I not seen her in very long time.' Again his face clouded over and Josh sensed that he was holding something back. Perhaps he was simply being tactful and didn't want to upset Josh with details of a romance, which in truth, could well have unhinged him at that precise moment. The thought of her finding love with someone else, illogical as it was, would ruin this incredible image he was seeing before him.

They left the restaurant exchanging email addresses, with warm promises to keep in touch. Back at the hotel they immediately searched the internet for the name Yakira. Links appeared immediately, complete with clips and photos giving details of her upcoming performances.

'She certainly has a tireless schedule,' Alistair commented as he read out the list. 'Sunday 17th November

Paris. Wednesday 20th Helsinki. Sunday 24th Munich. Tuesday 26th Vaduz. Thursday 28th Berlin. Sunday 1st December Tel Aviv'

'Tel Aviv!' Josh repeated with exuberance. 'That would give me ample time to travel home from here and then fly to Tel Aviv for "further business."

'Well I've never been to Israel,' Alistair put in, 'but it's on my wish list and I certainly don't intend to miss out on the fun. I'll return to Rome, then book a flight to Tel Aviv as well. You know, when I saw Yang's portrait in her mother's home I vaguely recognized her, but had no reason to connect her to Yakira.'

The concert was to take place in Tel Aviv's largest concert hall, the Charles Bronfman Auditorium. However when they tried to buy tickets online, to their disappointment it was completely sold out.

'I've a friend in Israel in the music business and he can perform miracles,' Josh told him. 'I'll email him and ask if he can possibly find two seats for us. He achieved what I had always wanted to do. He came to live in Israel when his children were young enough to bring them without disruption to their schooling.'

'Did he know about Yang?'

'Yes, in fact he was the only one of my friends who did know. We met when we were both studying at yeshiva in Jerusalem. Together we were partners in crime, sneaking off from lessons to go into town for a burger. Back in England and at university we kept in touch from time to time, but we lost contact when he moved to Israel. When I knew I was going to be working there, I managed to reconnect with him and we became close friends again. Since he didn't know Miriam I wasn't compromising his loyalties and I knew I could trust him totally, so I confided in him.'

'So perhaps you should tell him who Yakira really is.' Alistair suggested.

'Yes you are right; I owe that to him if I am going to ask for this favour.' His response came back speedily. Not only had he managed to book two seats but three, since he certainly intended to be there as well.

Chapter Nineteen

"Peace begins with a smile."
Mother Teresa

Friday 15th November 2019. Caye Caulker

By now Josh was used to Alistair's impersonations and theatrics. In fact he was never quite sure who would welcome him at breakfast. If he was greeted with the words "*it's good morning from me and it's good morning from him",* he knew he was going to be treated to Ronnie Corbett's distinctive voice. If on the other hand, he heard Prince Charles' cultured accent, he might expect an essay on architectural theories. Another day, it could be Mr Wong telling some dreadful jokes, but since discovering Josh's admiration for Sir Winston Churchill, Alistair often invited Winnie to make an appearance. "*The best argument against democracy is a five minute conversation with the average voter"* he quoted in a voice that resembled Winston's deep, gravelly tones with great accuracy.

Once they settled down to breakfast and Winston had been banished from the conversation, Josh put forward a suggestion.

'Since we aren't flying out before Sunday, would you fancy a Shabbat with Chabad?'

He went on to elaborate that Chabad was a very special branch of Chassidism, which had set up centres in far-reaching corners of the globe, providing Shabbat meals to Jewish travellers, no matter how far from home they might have journeyed.

'Do you know if there is one here?' Alistair asked with scepticism.

'Yes I've checked and Chabad is in Caye Caulker. We could take a ferry across this afternoon and stay there. Would that be okay?'

'Alistair readily agreed. 'I understand it's even more stunning than here. Although I am sure we will raise the average age considerably, as it appeals to young backpackers.'

'That is exactly the reason why Chabad would set up a centre there.'

The young rabbi and his family welcomed Alistair, Josh and an odd assortment of young vacationers to their Friday night meal. After the traditional songs of welcome and blessings over bread and wine, the chicken soup was served. Alistair was impressed to see how the entire family, even down to the three-year old, helped to serve.

No-one was in a hurry. A respite before the main course gave the rabbi an opportunity to welcome his guests and ask everyone to say a few words about themselves. This was a new and very different experience for Alistair, who was fascinated to hear that indeed the guests had come from all corners of the earth. The very substantial main course was served while Alistair wondered how they knew the numbers to cater for. They had not been asked to register for the meal. The family had simply opened their house to welcome all who came. Before the children brought on dessert, the rabbi told a short story from the Jewish sages.

'A rabbi, his heavily pregnant wife and their six children arrived in a small town somewhere in Eastern Europe, where he was due to take up a new posting. His wife was going to need help at home, so he decided to visit the good townsfolk to ask if they could recommend someone. It was also an opportunity to become acquainted with them. They all welcomed him with enthusiasm and were eager to give their suggestions for possible help, but without exception they all added their warning. "Whoever you take, just don't take Sarah the old crow." Each one added their own embellishment about her dreadful behaviour, how she cursed them and was belligerent and aggressive. They would chase her away in petrified fear if she came anywhere near their home or children. The rabbi, not wanting to initiate gossip, did not encourage these conversations. The feather story was always predominant in his mind. If you cut open a pillow, a cloud of feathers would spill out and float about the room, they would fly out of the window in a big swirling trail. No matter how far and how long you chased after the feathers, you could never put them all back, and so it was with gossip. Once out, you do not know where it will end. It flies on the wings of the wind and can't be halted.

His final visit was to a reclusive old lady, whose kind eyes peered out of a crumpled face when she opened the door. He posed the same question he had asked all the other congregants. Without hesitation she answered, *'Sarah, she is the sweetest, kindest person you could wish to meet. She walks here every week no matter the weather bringing my shopping and helping me in the house. She is an angel.'*

The rabbi thanked her for the advice and decided to go and meet Sarah, trying to fathom why all the good people of the town perceived her as a dragon, apart from one old lady who saw her as an angel.

Sarah opened the door of her tumble-down shack suspiciously. Once he introduced himself, she invited him in revealing one lone tooth as she smiled in welcome. Disfigured, with long grey matted hair, she was an altogether alarming apparition. It immediately became clear to the wise rabbi why all the townsfolk despised her. They judged her by her appearance and treated her badly, which must have hurt her deeply and in turn invoked her bad behaviour. The only person who showed kindness to her was rewarded by being the beneficiary of Sarah's true nature.'

Finishing his parable, the Rabbi lovingly chanted grace after the meal, quite unperturbed that almost the only person joining in apart from his family was Josh. As everyone took their leave he told them the time for Shabbat morning prayers, adding that whether they came or not, they were invited for lunch, when his wife's delicious cholent would be served.

Walking the short distance back to their hotel, Alistair was curious to learn more about these incredibly open hearted people.

'The name Chabad is an acronym formed from three Hebrew words *Chochmah, Bina and Da'at* which translates as wisdom, understanding and knowledge,' Josh elucidated. 'This represents their basic philosophy, which manifests itself in their outreach policy. They don't try to indoctrinate, but reach out to Jews of all affiliations, to encourage their participation in Jewish life wherever they might be. When a rabbi and his family are sent to one of these remote places, he sees it as his calling and embraces it unconditionally, usually staying for a number of years until his Rabbi should see fit for him to move on. Do you want to go back tomorrow for the cholent?' Josh enquired.

'Most definitely! This is a unique experience for me.'

Chapter Twenty

"I destroy my enemies when I make them my friends."
Abraham Lincoln

Saturday 16th November 2019. Caye Caulker

The following day, Shabbat, the Chabad rabbi greeted Josh, Alistair and all the other guests just like old friends, telling them he was overjoyed to see them again. Without any attempt to preach to his guests, he spoke for a few minutes about the Torah reading and then went round the table asking everyone to share an insight from their holiday.

A young man, who had introduced himself the previous night as Jules from Australia, spoke about his vocation as a naturalist and editor of an online diving magazine. His numerous tattoos, gold and silver body attachments and Rastafarian hairstyle belied his eloquent and cultured voice. It made Josh think about the moral of the Rabbi's story, not to judge a book by its cover.

Jules told them that he had come to Belize to do a comparative study between the Belize Reef and the Great Barrier Reef, since these were considered the two finest destinations for divers and ocean enthusiasts. He spoke reverently about the stunning underwater flora and fauna and described his encounters with sharks, massive sea turtles and a great variety of other breath-taking marine creatures.

'How do the two reefs compare?' the Rabbi enquired with interest.

'Belize is a much more concentrated experience and the Great Blue hole is one of the most famous dive sites.'

'I understand it is over 400 feet deep,' one of the other guests added, 'can you dive into it?'

'Yes since I am considered an underwater veteran I am allowed to explore it, but only to a certain depth. That was one of the most incredible experiences of my life.' He paused then added 'and *this* is another one…….thank you so much for enabling me to partake in these Shabbat meals with you. Although I am not religious, the culture and traditions of our religion, especially surrounding Shabbat are very important to me. You have both made me feel at home.' The Rabbi's wife was clearly touched by his words.

'Comments like that make it all worthwhile for us.'

She then asked him 'did you know that the Great Hole was visited and written about by both Jacque Cousteau and Charles Darwin?' The lively and spirited conversation went on round the crowded table, until reluctantly the guests began to disperse, not wanting to overstay their welcome.

After Shabbat, Josh and Alistair transferred to a hotel in Belize City for their last evening, in order to leave in good time for their flights. Josh was flying to London via Miami, before setting out again with more excuses, for the concert in Tel Aviv. Alistair was also flying to Miami, since there was no direct flight from Belize to the Cayman Islands. They knew that this would be the last instalment of their escapades, which had included a few perilous incidents, but mostly unforgettable highlights.

They went to the bar for a final farewell drink. Sitting in an armchair, Josh was deep in melancholy and wistful thoughts at the prospect of their imminent parting. He hardly registered the time Alistair was taking to bring over the drinks, but when Josh glanced up, Alistair was ambling jauntily towards him. He held a tray where three drinks perched precariously and he was chatting enthusiastically to an elegant stranger in fluent Italian

Unable to conceal his excitement, Alistair introduced Josh to Luigi DaVinci. 'I overheard him making inquiries in Italian and couldn't resist interrupting. Not only does Luigi live in Rome, he also collects snuff bottles!'

'My collection is very modest,' Luigi pointed out, as he joined them at the table. He was clearly fascinated to hear more about Alistair's collection.

'Would you like to see the book which I published for the exhibition?'

Encouraged by Luigi's obvious interest, he went back to his bedroom for his book. He lovingly and laboriously opened the box, revealing the prized edition. Luigi was completely transfixed by it, quietly reading while Josh and Alistair made their final plans. When they stood up to take their leave, Luigi relinquished the book with obvious reluctance.

'Would there be any chance of holding on to it till the morning? I'm a night bird and would love to spend more time looking at it.'

'With pleasure,' Alistair readily agreed. 'You can give it back to me at breakfast.'

Josh was aghast that Alistair was willing to trust this stranger with his book and precious snuff bottle. The book could be replaced, but Josh knew that the bottle embedded in the cover page had deep sentimental value to Alistair, as his father had bought it for him all those years ago. For all his worldliness, Alistair was naive and trusting.

Chapter Twenty-One

"This above all: to thine own self be true."
Polonius in William Shakespeare's Hamlet

Sunday 17th November 2019. Belize City

At breakfast the following morning Josh looked around the dining room, in what he was sure would be a futile search for Luigi. He relayed his fears to Alistair who was unfazed. With total faith he had no doubt that Luigi had merely overslept.

'If he doesn't appear by the time we finish breakfast I'll call his room.'

Just as they were leaving the dining room, much to Josh's surprise, his fears were allayed when Luigi strode in their direction, greeting Alistair with grateful thanks, as he handed over the box. They held a lengthy conversation in demonstrative Italian, accompanied by lots of hand waving, before they took leave of each other with a kiss on both cheeks and an exchange of phone numbers.

Alistair was in high spirits on the journey to the airport and Josh asked him what he and Luigi had discussed.

'He said that he would like to contact me when we are both back in Rome, as he would love to see my collection.' Josh couldn't help but question if snuff bottles were the only interest they had in common.

At the busy airport, Josh began to feel maudlin at the prospect of his imminent departure.

'Alistair, I really don't know how to thank you. It has been an amazing experience, one I would never have done without your encouragement. Not only have I benefited from an exceptional holiday, we even tracked down Yang. I am sorry that you didn't have any success with your own pursuits.'

'In Oscar's words "*Life cheats us with shadows. We ask it for pleasure. It gives it to us with bitterness and disappointment in its train.*"

Worry not my friend, for I have profited immensely from our truly momentous odyssey and rejoice in your triumphs. Now I am looking forward to meeting up again in Tel Aviv for our grand finale.'

Waiting at security, they were unaware of a sniffer dog which was paying particular attention to Alistair's suitcase. Alistair complied with the security guard's surly order to open it and was horrified when he pulled the lid roughly off his precious box. He was even more aghast when the guard examined the book, brandishing a knife about to cut open the front cover.

Pleading with him not to ruin his book, Alistair showed them how to remove the perspex cover. As he did so, Alistair was mortified to see a cascade of white powder escape. Immediately he was surrounded by a swarm of guards. Josh watched in dismay as Alistair vehemently protested his ignorance. The truth dawned on Josh, who was sure that the suave Luigi DaVinci must have been behind it. He tried to explain this to the officers and beseeched them to call the hotel in an endeavour to apprehend him.

A grim-faced officer returned a few minutes later, telling Alistair they would have to take him to the holding centre at the local police station. There was no record of anyone by that name registered at the hotel. Despite Josh's protestations and insistence that he could corroborate his story, Alistair was led away with a petrified expression on his face. Above the raucous hubbub, Alistair managed to shout the name of his Italian lawyer in Josh's direction. Amidst the chaos Josh promised to return to the hotel, call the lawyer as well as The British Consul, the Italian Consul and even his own law firm to intervene on Alistair's behalf. Before leaving the airport he went to the airline desk to explain the circumstances and yet again reschedule his flight.

After numerous stressful phone calls, Josh was assured that the British High Commissioner to Belize would try to secure Alistair's release.

'He won't last a night with all those murderers in there,' Josh implored them, but he was told that it was doubtful they would manage to do anything before morning.

Josh went down to breakfast bleary-eyed the next morning after a fitful night's sleep. A waiter brought him some much-needed coffee, asking 'where is your friend this morning?' Josh told him the terrible story.

'Perhaps I can help,' he offered. 'I saw you both sitting with that Italian last night and I noticed that your friend was showing him the book. I also happened to notice him returning the book to him at breakfast.' He then added slightly sheepishly 'I was watching because I was a little envious. Before your friend appeared, I was chatting to the Italian and I must admit I rather liked him. So that's why I was taking such an interest.'

'Would you be willing to come with me to the police station to tell them this?' Josh asked eagerly.

'Certainly' he agreed.

Chapter Twenty Two

"Everybody is a genius.
But if you judge a fish by its ability to climb a tree,
it will live its whole life believing that it is stupid ."
Albert Einstein

Monday 18th November 2019. Belize City

Once the waiter had given his testament and with the intervention of the High Commissioner, Alistair, looking none the worse for his temporary incarceration, was released together with his cherished book. Making their way back to the hotel in a taxi Josh listened incredulously, as Alistair recounted the experience. Far from being traumatized by such a horrific nightmare, he appeared quite calm, almost jocular.

'You must have been petrified to have been locked up with all those thugs; I bet you didn't sleep for a second. I know I lay awake all night worrying about you and worrying about your precious snuff bottle, knowing how much it means to you.'

'You didn't need to worry on either account,' Alistair chuckled, 'thanks to my impersonations; they were all too busy laughing to molest me.'

'Did they know any of the characters?'

'No but that didn't matter, they still found them funny. As far as my snuff bottle is concerned, I might have omitted to mention to you that it is just a copy. The original is safely secured at home in Rome.

I was in a cell with four others and yes, it was frightening, but also an insight. A fourteen year-old boy was in there for murder. He told me that his parents had abandoned him, leaving no alternative but to live on the streets, and little choice but to join a gang. In order to show that he was worthy to join, he first had to prove himself by committing a random murder. Many of these kids don't want this life but most of them have no alternative, they are born into it. Mungo, our taxi-driver, was one of the lucky ones who did manage to escape, but who knows for how long? The police crackdown and consequently many young boys simply languish in prison.'

Back at the hotel, after a few hours catching up on their sleep they met up in the bar. Alistair greeted Josh in a buccaneer's voice. 'Me ole mate Joshua how would you fancy joining me for the pirate festival in the Cayman Islands?' Not having a clue what Alistair was talking about, Josh waited for him to elaborate.

'You have already missed your plane home, and since your brush with death at the tender age of twelve involved piracy, how about accompanying me to the Cayman Islands? A pirate carnival takes place there every year during November. We could extend our adventures together and I could then accompany you to Tel Aviv.'

To continue their travels, to witness re-enactments of pirate roguery, to relive his childhood fantasies, the notion was almost too delicious to contemplate. 'Let's go.' he said, before he was aware that he had even spoken the words aloud. After all, he reflected, this would be his last fling before returning to his life of conformity and compliance. When he had impulsively booked the trip to Shanghai he could never have envisioned where his search would lead him.

'Splendid' Alistair responded, 'that's settled, I'll check flights. Alternatively, there is another option, he added with a duplicitous look on his face.'

'Alistair! Having travelled with you for nearly three weeks, nothing you suggest would shock me.'

'Good! What would you say about a cruise?' He paused for a moment to give Josh time to digest the idea. 'Fortuitously it happens that a ship is docking in Belize tomorrow. It is coming from Fort Lauderdale before sailing on to Belize, Jamaica and the Cayman Islands, then returning to Fort Lauderdale.'

'Jamaica!' Josh burst out loudly. 'There were Jewish pirates operating in the Caribbean during the seventeenth century and I know that some are buried in a very old Jewish cemetery in Kingston. Jamaica is also where Ian Fleming wrote many of his novels and to top all that, it's Bob Marley's birthplace. It would be incredible if we could go.'

Sounding just like an eager schoolboy he added in disbelief. 'Going on this cruise would make two of my childhood dreams come true, to go to Jamaica and to go on a cruise. On the few occasions I suggested it to Miriam she was totally dismissive, considering it too secular.

Let's call and see if they accept new passengers' en-route and if they have two single cabins.' A doubt then occurred to him as he wondered if Alistair would have enough time to deal with his finances. 'How long will the ship be in the Cayman Islands? Will it be long enough for you to finish all your business?'

'Yes worry not; the financial business is of less consequence. Sebastian has been dealing admirably with my portfolio for many years. It's long overdue that I make his acquaintance.

Josh could hardly contain himself when the cruise line informed Alistair that they had some empty cabins, and would be willing to allow them to embark in Belize. Alistair seemed as excited as Josh at the prospect. Once again he quoted Oscar.

"One can live for years sometimes without living at all, and then all life comes crowding into a single hour."

'Not sure about an hour, but certainly a month' Josh agreed.

Now for Josh, all that remained was the small matter of explaining to Miriam the necessity of a cruise, in order to complete a business deal!

Chapter Twenty Three

"When one door of happiness closes, another opens,
but often we look so long at the closed door
that we do not see the one that has been opened for us."
Helen Keller

Tuesday 19th November 2019. Caribbean Cruise

Although the cruise had started at Fort Lauderdale, a few passengers had boarded at Belize. They were invited to attend a reception, where they were greeted by a pretty stewardess handing out drinks and joking with the passengers. The purser went over the emergency evacuation plan, which he assured them had never been put to the test. He then collected their passports in exchange for Sea Pass cards, to be used at each port, promising their return at the end of the voyage.

'Ensuring that we are not left with any stowaways,' he joked. 'A daily bulletin sheet will appear on your bed each evening to guide you through the next day's fun and games,' adding with a broad grin 'and the crew of this floating paradise are here to ensure that it will all be plain sailing from now on.'

With all the embarkation formalities completed and Josh settled in his cabin or Stateroom as it was called, he had to pinch himself in disbelief. What madness had taken over his brain to bring him halfway round the world and now, on a cruise to Jamaica and the Cayman Islands? Was he a hypocrite? If his congregation or family were ever to find out about the closet life he had led, not to mention his infractions of the religious laws, they would be horrified. He would be castigated, but would that be justified?

Sometimes he tried to rationalise his actions, telling himself that at least he had never misled Yang. He knew he was far from the first man to have an affair. Many did, promising their lover that in time they would leave their wives. He had never lied to Yang and had always made it abundantly clear that ultimately, there was no future for their life together. He would never leave his family.

How many others were pulled in opposite directions? How many men and women tried to juggle the contradictions secretly consuming their very being? Did it make him such a bad person, when all he had done was try and steal a small piece of happiness for himself, without causing pain to those who loved and valued him? He tried to help people less fortunate than himself and would never refuse to give charity whatever the cause. However, no matter how much he tried to justify his behaviour, he knew that his family and community would not make the slightest concession with regard to his misdeeds. He would be thought of as cruel, heartless and even evil. He had seen it happen to others who had been lambasted for lesser misdemeanours.

Just before five, Josh and Alistair made their way to one of the entertainment lounges where they combined as an impressive team, easily winning the trivia quiz, before freshening up for dinner. According to the itinerary, dining-room attire was "sundown chic." Josh had only packed for a week and he was beginning to wish he had brought more clothes. Alistair always managed to look debonair and stylish. Josh was beginning to feel quite shabby in comparison.

As they queued outside the dining room, he observed that he didn't have to worry. It seemed that almost anything was acceptable, as long as it wasn't a swimsuit or bathrobe. Some ladies were resplendently overstated in jewels and sequins, whilst others were smart but more casual.

Their designated table was already occupied by a couple, who seemed to be oblivious to the surroundings as they gazed lovingly into each other's eyes. They looked up to greet their dinner companions and Josh gave out a blood-curdling shriek "YANG." Diners watched in fascination as the couple reacted with blank looks and shocked silence. Josh immediately realised his error. She was young, stunning and Chinese, transfixing Josh by her startling resemblance to Yang. Quickly regaining his composure, he apologised for his mistake.

The couple laughed and introduced themselves as Dee and Damien Montague. Damien informed them happily that he must be the luckiest South African alive, on honeymoon with his beautiful Macanese wife. Dee was presumably much younger than Damien, but they seemed to share the same sort of adoration that he had shared with Yang, evoking an immediate affinity towards them. Whilst Alistair chatted easily, Josh's mind wandered to a secluded area of the ship, where he was embracing Dee. Except, Dee evolved into Yang. Josh emerged from his insane fantasy when Damien ordered a second drink and Dee's voice took on a sharp edge.

'Darling, I think you have had enough,'

'I will decide that,' he replied, trying to hide his irritation.

'Doctors orders' Dee offered as explanation, 'gout, he needs to keep his uric acid levels down.'

'These good people don't need to hear my medical history' he retorted tersely.

In an attempt to relieve the tension Alistair inquired where they had met.

'In the casino of the MGM Cotai hotel in Macau' Dee responded. 'We just happened to be sitting side by side at one of the gaming tables.'

'Not only did she win triumphantly at the tables, she also won my heart.'

Equilibrium restored, they continued to reminisce about their whirlwind romance. At the end of the meal Dee suggested that Josh and Alistair join them in the casino. Both declined, but expressed a hope that they would have another opportunity to sit together.

Chapter Twenty Four

"The sea, once it casts its spell,
holds one in its net of wonder forever."
Jacques Yves Cousteau

Wednesday 20th November 2019. At Sea

Over breakfast, Josh and Alistair studied the day's program, which ranged from competitions to dance lessons, glass making, bingo and lectures on a myriad of fascinating subjects. They each marked those they deemed the most interesting events. Given such a diverse program, they agreed to follow their own agendas, meeting up for the trivia quiz at five.

Josh decided to spend time acquainting himself with the many varied amenities on board. He would start from the top - deck fifteen, and work his way down. Surprisingly, the top deck held little other than a chapel, but descending the stairs to deck fourteen he encountered a multitude of pursuits, including water slides, rock climbing, ice rink, a bowling alley and a gym. He could have easily spent the whole day on that deck alone had he been a little younger. Decks thirteen and twelve included children's adventure areas, a running track and fitness centre, bars, coffee corners and ice cream wagons scattered throughout. Descending the stairs to each deck, he wandered past swimming pools, Jacuzzis of all shapes and sizes, gourmet restaurants, and a self-service area offering every conceivable cuisine. Arriving on the eighth floor, the well-stocked library beckoned him in to inspect its prolific writers. To his pleasure, he found some volumes by Winston Churchill. The inviting armchair and serene surroundings were so seductive that he became quite lost in Winston's erudite words, until, noticing the large clock, became aware that he had spent the whole morning reading. He could do that at home; he scolded himself, as he hastily returned the book to its place on the shelf.

The energy and dynamism of the ship was centred around decks three, four and five, where shows, casinos and other entertainment took place with frenetic action. The formal dining room with waiter service spanned all three floors. As Josh came down to deck five he wandered through the main thoroughfare, lined with shops and galleries selling top-of-the-range brands.

Walking past the art gallery, he recognized a familiar Chinese plait and went in to discover what fortunes Alistair was probably spending. Greeting Josh with an unrestrained gesture of delight, Alistair pointed to the artwork he was admiring. It was a Chinese painting of a Shih Tzu dog, which matched the one depicted on his snuff bottle. The painting would be in the auction taking place that evening and he had registered both their names in order to participate.

'In case you wish to buy your wife a painting,' he added with a mischievous smile. 'How about this one?' he asked, pointing to the iconic image of Albert Einstein with his hair in its distinctive disarray and tongue sticking out.

'It would only appeal to Miriam if it was an eminent Rabbi' Josh commented with a hint of sadness creeping into his voice. Noticing the time, they raced off to take their places for the quiz. They had designated themselves Oscar and Winnie and it came as no surprise to the rest of the contestants when Oscar and Winnie were proclaimed the winners again.

Sitting down at a table by the window of the enormous dining room that evening, they were joined by a bevy of four attractive, blond ladies. A certain symmetry between the four could have indicated that they were sisters, had it not been for the obvious disparity in their ages, which seemed to range somewhere between twenty and eighty. Three of them were dressed in modest, but fashionable outfits. This was quite at variance with the outrageously captivating attire of the youngest. A long-sleeved, lace crop-top revealed a flower tattooed just above her midriff. A mini skirt, high boots and a green streak running through her otherwise blond curls completed the exotic image.

Alistair, with his irrepressible humour, asked 'Sisters?' eliciting identical peals of laughter. They all tried to speak at once, but deferred to the oldest as their spokeswoman. 'We are four generations of the same family. I am known as GG, as I don't like to be referred to as Great-Grandma. This is my daughter Julie, my granddaughter Sam and great granddaughter Fleur. She was the winner of a television talent competition a few years ago and has become a phenomenal super-star.'

'Oh GG' she said modestly 'that is a bit of an exaggeration.'

'On the contrary, it's quite true and well-deserved. Undeterred, she continued 'Fleur was invited to be the celebrity singer on board and as a special treat for my 80th birthday, invited all of us to join her. She wrote in her invitation, "a mother is a daughter's best friend" so she couldn't think of anyone better to share this experience with.' GG produced three photos with the face in each picture resembling Fleur's. 'Here we all are at the age Fleur is now.' Undeniably, they had all been great beauties.

The rest of the meal was spent in relaxed conversation. Leaving the table, Alistair with his endearing charm, told the ladies that a herd of wild horses would not keep them away from Fleur's concert.

Alistair's exuberance was infectious as they made their way to the art gallery for the auction. He told Josh that the picture was one of a limited edition. It was a copy of an eighteenth century painting by Giuseppe Castiglione. Had it been an original, it would sell for millions. Josh was beginning to think that even that sort of price would not daunt Alistair.

On entering the auditorium, they were greeted by the Park West Gallery representative who checked them off her list and gave them each an auction paddle. Taking their seats and waiting for the auction to start, they were offered sparkling white wine. Josh picked up the catalogue whilst Alistair, in his customary friendly manner, initiated a conversation with his neighbour.

There was much preamble by the auctioneer, intended to set the participants at ease and motivate positive purchasing energy with his patter.

'Good evening everyone. I hope you are all psyched up and ready to go. Do you all have your paddles or weapons as I call them? Lift them up. As long as I can see them I am a satisfied man.' Alistair groaned at the chatter, becoming even more impatient when an ensemble appeared and launched into the song "Run-around Sue".

'Get on with it' Alistair grumbled.

The auctioneer's assistant finally came on with the first painting. It was a scene of Venice, with a pretty lady smiling enigmatically as she rode in a gondola.

'Isn't she charming?' It took a few seconds for his audience to appreciate that the auctioneer was actually referring to his assistant, not to the painting. He gushed 'We met on a cruise, married on a cruise and work together on a cruise. Are we ready? Lot three hundred.' After a detailed description of the painting, in a flurry of unintelligible auctioneers jargon he started the bidding, which was completed in a fast-paced whirl. 'Last chance, going, going, gone,' he banged his wooden gavel on his podium.

The painting which held Alistair's interest was displayed, after what seemed to him like an interminable age. 'Here we have a copy of a painting of a Shih Tzu dog, one of the favourite hounds of the Qianlong Emperor - isn't he just adorable? This is a numbered copy of a painting in the style of the Italian master, Giuseppe Castiglione, who was a missionary in China, also serving as an artist at the Imperial Court. He was especially praised for his portraits of dogs. This is a stylized landscape of flowers and flowering bushes, with the dog gazing up at the bird perching on one of the branches. Landscape painting was regarded as the highest form of Chinese art, which draws on Chinese heritage and culture to tell its story.'

'Yes, yes we know all that' Josh could hear Alistair muttering under his breath.

'Who will start the bidding for this limited edition?' Immediately someone's paddle went up and the pace took momentum, quickly reaching its reserve. Finally a determined Alistair managed to outbid all competition, acquiring the coveted painting for a sum which staggered Josh. Alistair, enchanted by his purchase, was quite unperturbed at the cost.

After a number of modern art works were sold, a much smaller painting was shown which kindled Josh's interest when referred to as a copy of a painting by Sir Winston Churchill. Entitled *"Villa on the Nivelle"* the original had been painted in 1945.

The auctioneer called out 'going once, going twice,' and to Josh's own amazement, his hand took on a life of its own as he raised his paddle and put in a bid of one thousand dollars. The gavel descended. 'Sold at a bargain price of one thousand dollars.'

Alistair offered his congratulations, adding that Oscar would have approved.

"Modern pictures - one exhausts what they have to say in a very short time, and then they become as tedious as one's relations."

'I'll hang it in my study, above the table with the humidor holding Winnie's cigar. It will be the perfect memento of this unforgettable holiday.'

Once all the fervour had subsided Alistair introduced Josh to the lady on his other side, with whom he had been chatting. 'Josh, this lovely lady is Esther and she is giving an art class tomorrow afternoon after our visit to Jamaica.'

'As much as I would love to paint and love looking at art,' Josh declared, 'I am totally incapable of creating it. I was always bottom of my art class at school.'

'In that case you are the perfect candidate for my class' Esther said with conviction. 'Come along and I'll prove you wrong.'

'What time is the class?'

'Six o'clock in the art studio, deck twelve. You have to be back on board by then because we sail at five. Hope to see you both,' she added with a disarming smile as she looked at her watch and hurried off.

Chapter Twenty Five

"I have come to believe that this is a mighty continent which was hitherto unknown."
Christopher Columbus

Thursday 21st November 2019. Ocho Rios

Today Josh would fulfil another childhood dream - to visit Jamaica. In order to be back in time for sailing at five, they agreed to hire a taxi for the day. Recalling their frightening experience in Belize, they paid extra heed to warnings of lurking dangers and asked the purser's assistant to book a reputable driver for them.

Throughout the twenty minute drive along the northern coastline to Oracabessa Bay, the driver interspersed his knowledgeable commentary by singing along with Bob Marley songs, which were playing in the background.

"Hear the children crying one love,
Hear the children crying one heart."

'Ian Fleming originally named his estate "Goldeneye," after a military operation in which he was involved. He built it in 1946 on the edge of a cliff overlooking the beach. Lots of reggae concerts are held there and it has even been renamed "James Bond Beach."

"One love, one heart,
Let's get together and feel all right."

It's now a private hotel. If you like, I can take you there and you can rent the main house for two thousand five hundred dollars a night,' yet again bursting into song,

"Old pirates yes they rob I
Sold I to the merchant ships.
Minutes after they took I
From the bottomless pit"

'In 1952 Fleming began writing his first Bond novel Casino Royale and for the next twelve years he wrote all his Bond stories there."

As they drove round the area they could well perceive how the dramatic landscape, lush tropical foliage, shimmering blue sea and stunning backdrops had inspired Fleming in his novels.

Leaving the idyllic scenery of Oracabessa Bay, they headed south to Kingston where they turned off the road and through gates into the colourful forecourt of the Bob Marley Museum. The life-size bronze sculpture and gigantic murals of Marley left them in no doubt as to his immense stature. They entered the nineteenth century dwelling which had been his modest home for many years. Before the guide led them through the house she asked them to join in singing "*One Love*" which was playing in the background.

'This song,' she informed them, 'symbolized Bob's basic philosophy, which was that all differences be put aside, and everyone should be united. Although he was raised as a Catholic he converted to Rastafari. Their beliefs include wearing their hair in its natural long uncombed state. Hence, the emergence of his famous dreadlocks.'

Throughout the tour reggae music played in the background. The guide spoke about the assassination attempt on Marley's life and the numerous children he had fathered, before dying at the young age of thirty six. She mentioned his mother Cedella, his siblings and his children all of whom were very musical.

Fascinated by the many artefacts, they had hardly noticed the time slipping by. They left hurriedly for their next destination.

'What she didn't tell us' Josh added as they walked out, 'is that his father was a white Jamaican whose family claimed to have Syrian Jewish origins,'

As soon as Josh knew that they would be visiting Kingston, he had emailed the Sha'are Shalom Community, asking if it would be possible to have a guided tour of the Synagogue and the Hunts Bay cemetery. They had replied that one of their members, Jacob Kovetski would be able to show them around and would look forward to meeting them there.

Indeed, the Synagogue was a large and impressive edifice. Jacob pointed out that the floor was covered in sand from the Sephardi custom, a reminder of the Spanish Inquisition, when Jews had to cover their floors with sand to muffle the sound of their prayers.

'Although we were once an Orthodox community,' he told them, 'we are now affiliated to the Reform branch of Judaism.' He led them into the adjacent museum, which he informed them proudly, was considered one of the finest historical collections in the Caribbean.

Since Jacob lived near Ocho Rios, he offered to drive Josh and Alistair to the cemetery and return them to the cruise ship in good time for sailing at five. They gratefully accepted his offer, especially as their own taxi driver had no idea where the cemetery was situated. Eventually they arrived at the graveyard, which was partially hidden at the end of a dusty lane, almost at the water's edge, in a refuse-strewn area. As they wandered through weed-covered rows of cracked headstones, Josh managed to decipher Hebrew writing under the skull and crossbones symbol.

Jacob filled in some background. 'We're actually standing in a landmark of rare historical interest. It is one of the oldest Jewish cemeteries in the Western Hemisphere and resting place to a number of roguish buccaneers. Thanks to Christopher Columbus, the Island of Jamaica became a place of refuge for many Sephardi Jews following their expulsion from Spain and Portugal. Columbus was granted dominion over the whole island by the Spanish crown and he decreed it free from the inquisition. His motives have been the subject of much speculation' Jacob added, citing various publications on the subject.

'In the aftermath of the inquisition, a group of swashbuckling Jews roamed the high seas in ships with names like Queen Esther, The Prophet Samuel and Shield of Abraham. They attacked the Spanish fleet in retribution for the terrible treatment meted out to their brethren.'

Looking at his watch, Jacob pointed out that time was running short. I'll save stories of the most notorious Jewish pirates for our return journey.'

Josh and Alistair piled into Jacob's old jalopy to head back to the ship. Driving along, he regaled them with thrilling tales of marauding pirates and banditry.

'One of the more colourful pirates around at the time was Rabbi Shmuel Panache, who decided that life as a pirate was more thrilling than that of a rabbi. The story goes that he used to travel with his own kosher chef and he had the sign of a phoenix attached to the front of his ship. This was to symbolize that although individual Jews could be destroyed, as a people they would rise again.

Then there was Moses Cohen Henriques.'

'Your friend' Alistair interjected to Josh.

'You heard about him?' Jacob asked Josh.

'Yes, I read that he plundered the modern day equivalent of almost one billion dollars from a Spanish galleon.'

They were so immersed in the remarkable and gripping stories recounted by Jacob that they didn't notice the smoke emerging from the car's engine, but could hardly miss it when clouds began to billow out. The car lumbered on valiantly for a few minutes becoming progressively slower, until it gave a loud choke before its final extinction.

Josh and Alistair were horrified. They had been well-warned of the dire consequences of missing the boat. Every information sheet contained a clear warning that if a passenger did not return before sailing time, it was his own personal responsibility to re-join the ship at the next port of call. Exacerbating their anxieties, they had also been warned of the crime rate in Jamaica, which ruled out the idea of hitching a ride, even if there had been any traffic in sight.

Jacob was full of profuse apologies, as he tried to call a friend to come and rescue them, but as he pointed out, phone reception in the area was patchy and spasmodic. Eventually, he managed to contact his friend who promised to come, but the time was slipping away, and their five o clock deadline was looming in front of them as a daunting curfew.

The minutes ticked away as they waited for Jacob's friend to arrive, but after frantic attempts to contact him again, it was obvious that the friend had not caught the full conversation. Consequently, he didn't appreciate the urgency of their situation and had not yet even left home. In the meantime, Alistair tried to call the cruise ship to explain their predicament, not that he expected them to delay sailing especially for them, but either way, he had no more luck than Jacob with the phone connection.

Standing in the middle of the road deliberating their options, they could hardly contain their elation when a taxi appeared and they recognized their original driver, who had stopped for refreshments in Kingston. ‘Yet again we are delivered out of the jaws of danger’ Alistair commented. ‘We must thank Saint Fiacre, the patron saint of taxi drivers.’

‘And I thought I was the font of useless knowledge’ Josh retorted.

Boarding the ship with minutes to spare they bumped into Damien, another last minute straggler, but on his own. He told them that Dee had decided to stay in Jamaica, as a friend was having a serious operation there and she wanted to be on-hand to help. She would fly to Fort Lauderdale to meet him after the cruise.

Despite their strenuous and emotionally-charged day, they didn’t want to miss their daily quiz date, which proved to be another victory for team Winnie and Oscar.

Josh then asked with resignation ‘So where is the art class taking place?’ As they walked in they were greeted by Esther and both shown to an easel.

When all the easels were occupied Esther began.

‘How many of you think you can’t draw?’

Almost everyone raised their hands.

'Well, I say that's a delusion and I am going to prove that everyone is capable of making some simple drawings. We aren't talking about Leonardo da Vinci painting the Mona Lisa, but rather something light-hearted to impress your grandchildren. Would you like to be able to draw these little characters?' As she asked, she lifted up the front page on her easel to show six cute cartoon figures. Everyone nodded their heads and she asked them to follow, step-by-step.

'First we draw a nose, something of an open, bulbous shape, then we add the eyes above. Little shapes like sixty-sixes or speech marks. Underneath the nose we add a curved line to make the mouth, displaying a nice big smile. Ok so far so good. Now, to the right add an open circle for the ear. Surround it with spikes for some hair. Add one line coming down from the left and another coming down under the ear. Join those two lines with a line to make the neck of a tee-shirt and here we have him.'

Everyone clapped in appreciation as they looked at their own achievements.

As they waited outside the doors of the Emerald Restaurant, Alistair, with his quirky geniality launched into his impersonations, amusing the two ladies standing behind them in the queue. They told him that he must enter the ship's talent contest. Easy conversation ensued and it was quite natural for the four of them to find a table together.

The two genteel English ladies introduced themselves with old-fashioned courtesy. When they revealed that they were the owners of a tattoo parlour in Brighton, for once Alistair's natural repartee was stymied in wonderment and disbelief. Explaining that originally they met at Art College, they bonded over a mutual fascination for the art of tattooing. Remaining friends throughout their respective careers, they recognised the increasing trend amongst young girls to have tattoos. They cited the misogyny in the industry as the driving force behind opening their own salon, run solely by women for women. Far from being a seedy, back-street parlour, their salon had a refined, serene ambience.

Eager to hear more, Josh inquired about the most frequently requested designs.

'Some of the more popular symbols are flowers, feathers, butterflies and dragons, but recently famous quotes have been in demand.

'Such as?'

'Well a very popular one is "*If not now when.*"

Josh smiled with recognition. 'That quote actually played an instrumental role in propelling me on this trip. Well, that and Alistair' he added gratefully. 'Do you know its origin?'

'No' they answered in unison.

'It is a well-known rabbinical saying, attributed to Hillel the Elder.'

If I am not for myself, who will be for me? If I am only for myself, what am I? If not now, when?"

Silence ensued while they pondered the words until Alistair spoke.

'I had a friend, who had a tattoo of an abacus on his hand,'

'Why?' they all asked in unison.

'He wanted his friends to know they could count on him.'

They groaned tolerantly at his joke.

After dinner, Josh and Alistair found their seats in the packed theatre. Fleur was introduced as one of Britain's most talented young singer songwriters, with a string of awards to her name. It soon became apparent that she deserved every accolade. Fleur's hauntingly melodious, rich powerful voice rang out throughout the auditorium to an enraptured audience. She accompanied herself alternately with guitar or piano. Throughout her performance, she chatted and joked easily with the audience, even asking if anyone would like to join her on stage to sing with her. When no one volunteered she told the crowd that someone very special had accompanied her on this cruise. To honour her eightieth birthday, she would like to invite her on stage to sing with her. GG, although taken aback, amidst encouraging cheers, joined Fleur on stage.

'GG let's sing your favourite song.' "*We'll meet again*" GG happily agreed.

It was clear that Fleur's great-grandma was no stranger to the stage. She gave a remarkable performance, as she proudly and lovingly sang and danced with her great granddaughter. It was evident that they were in perfect harmony, both on and off stage. When the concert ended, Josh and Alistair went over to the four generations who were talking together. They offered their praise, and asked if any of the ladies would like to join them for a drink. To their surprise all four accepted.

Seated in a quiet corner of the bar, the ladies took it in turns to sing old songs peppered with Alistair's impersonations. Suddenly, Grandma Julie exclaimed "*The two Alistairs"*. I remember your superb show at the Edinburgh Festival all those years ago.' As she reminisced, Josh sat back revelling in the moment. He had hardly given Miriam a thought throughout the trip but it occurred to him how different their lives could have been, if they were able to share such pleasurable times as these together.

Maybe he would reveal himself to Yang once the concert in Tel Aviv was over. Who knows, perhaps she still longed for him. He could live with her in Rome, become her manager and accompany her as she travelled round the world. The idea was delicious in its simplicity. If only, he sighed to himself. He knew he was indulging in an illusion of total absurdity.

He emerged from his ponderings to see that everyone was saying goodnight to each other, with the hope that in the words of Vera Lynn, they would meet again.

Chapter Twenty Six

"A person who never made a mistake
Never tried anything new."
Albert Einstein

Friday 22nd November 2019. Cayman Islands

The Pirate Festival was in full swing throughout the streets of Grand Cayman, with glittering parades, local live bands, crafts, entertainment and all forms of extravaganza. The highlight of the Festival was the Landing Pageant and float parade, during which a mock takeover of the Island by a band of fighting pirates was enacted. Josh imagined sharing this experience with Yang, as he soaked in the surroundings,

Returning to reality with a shudder, it occurred to him that he had not bought Miriam a gift. Was this simply because he had hidden her away in a closet for the holiday, or was he still subconsciously implementing his own disappearance?

Alistair made his way to the Bank to meet Sebastian, who then offered to accompany him in order to show him the best vantage points to enjoy the festivities. Without knowing how long matters would take, Alistair had not arranged to meet Josh, but inevitably they bumped into one another.

'Josh, this is Sebastian, my financial wizard.'

'Sebastian, this is Josh, my intrepid travel companion who tries to keep me out of harm's way.'

Smiling as he shook Josh's hand, Sebastian asked them what time they needed to be back on the ship.

'There is going to be a spectacular firework display over Harbour Drive this evening.' Sebastian informed them.

'Shame, but we nearly had our own fireworks yesterday, when we were almost left behind on the Jamaican shores. Hopefully we can watch it in the distance as we sail away.'

When Josh returned to his cabin, the itinerary for the next day was on his bed together with a bar of chocolate. Each evening a different treat awaited him.

On checking his itinerary for the evening's dress code (not that it made any difference since his wardrobe was exceedingly limited), he noticed that it included the prayer time for Friday night service in the synagogue. In a way perhaps Josh had been hoping for an unmistakable signal, which would lead him back onto the path of righteousness. The Bible was full of clear signs which had steered his forefathers on the right track. Was this his own sign, he wondered.

At the appropriate time, Josh made his way to one of the liner's smaller concert halls which had been allocated for the synagogue. He was a little disappointed by the sparse number of participants, barely a quorum, which for the purpose of the prayers was ten Jewish men over the age of thirteen. Gradually more latecomers arrived and prayer books were distributed. It became apparent that they were all waiting for someone else to start the service. Looking around, Josh could tell by the inappropriate attire, that few present were overtly religious. Most men were wearing the white skull cap bearing the ship's insignia, indicating they didn't have one of their own. He knew it was unlikely that any one of them was capable of taking the service, whereas Josh could do it blindfolded and knew it was his obligation to come forward.

Singing with gusto, he realised how much he enjoyed leading prayers and he could feel the vibes of appreciation. A sudden thought struck him. It was customary to say a few words on Friday night about the weekly Torah reading. He knew it was Chai Sarah - The Life of Sarah, so he delved into his memory to find some suitable sentiments.

At the end of the service, everyone congratulated him on his singing and inspiring words. They prevailed upon him to take the Shabbat morning service. Although he knew all the prayers and their melodies, reading the weekly Torah portion needed practice. He took a Chumash - The Five Books of Moses, which included each weekly portion, so that he could practice, but in his mind he thought "oh well, in the kingdom of the blind the one eyed man is king." Not one of Winnie's quotes but appropriate.

Everyone gradually dispersed, leaving one couple who lingered behind, evidently intent on speaking to Josh privately. Josh immediately recognized the wife as Esther, the art teacher. Her husband, who had been actively participating in the singing and prayers, could barely hide his emotions as he introduced himself to Josh.

'Harold Hart, but please call me Hal and I understand that you are already acquainted with Esther.' He continued excitedly, 'I must tell you that the last time I heard that tune for Lechu Dodi was when my grandfather sang it in Shul at my bar-mitzvah, shortly before he died. I've tried so many times to recall the melody, but have never heard it again till now.'

'It's our family tune! It originated in my father's hometown of Mannheim,' Josh elaborated.

'MANNHEIM' Hal exclaimed with incredulity, 'that's where my family came from.' The euphoric excitement and disbelief was tangible, as they both spoke at once about their families. Esther, who had been sharing her husband's jubilance, suggested that Josh and Alistair join them at their table for the Friday night meal to continue their conversation.

Meeting up outside the Emerald dining room, Esther and Hal were accompanied by four boys and a girl, all of whom were attired in pirate costumes. They were introduced as their grandchildren.

Comfortably seated, they asked Josh if he would lead them with his melodic voice. They sang the songs and blessings over wine and challah, the special bread they had asked the chef to prepare for them.

Alistair told them he was getting used to traditional Friday night meals and would miss them once he returned home. The couple said that they had always promised their five grandchildren that one year they would bring them to the Cayman Islands for the Pirate Festival. In an aside Hal added to Josh, 'Unfortunately, I recently received a rather worrying medical diagnosis, so we decided not to delay our promise any longer.'

Mentally Josh envisaged an absurd scene; he was on the cruise with Miriam and all nineteen grandchildren. The ludicrous picture it conjured up made him chuckle aloud, which seemed rather rude and unfeeling, just after Hal's comment about his medical condition. Josh apologized profusely, describing the ridiculous image. Again he had to admonish himself for allowing his fantasies to encroach upon reality.

He quickly changed the subject, asking the children if the Festival had been fun. Five voices answered in excited unison describing the pirate raid, the music, the costumes and most important of all, the costume contest. This had been won by the Hart's granddaughter Haylee, who had dressed as Captain Hook, complete with hand appendage, which she insisted on wearing throughout the meal, much to her grandmother's chagrin. It then became apparent why a life-size teddy bear was also sharing their table. Haylee proudly described the jubilant moment when she was pronounced winner and presented with the teddy bear.

Haylee, at eleven, was obviously the leader of the pack and chatted easily with self-confident poise.

'Teddy needs a name and I rather like the sound of Josh, so would you mind if I called him Joshy?' she asked, looking directly at him.

'I would be greatly flattered,' he replied. 'In fact, could we call him Joshy Boy? Someone I knew used to call me that.'

'Settled,' she said with resolve 'he will now be known as Joshy Boy. I am going to give him to my baby brother, who was too young to come on the cruise.'

Whilst waiting for their first course, Josh and Hal discussed their original family names and compared their parents' experiences. Hal's grandfather had recognized the dangers in the increasing deprivations inflicted on the Jews. He had managed to arrange for all his family to leave Germany in 1938, and sail to America to join his brother.

Josh told him that unfortunately the outcome of his family's story was not so fortuitous. His father, a teenager at the time, had been sent to England on the Kindertransport, never to see any of his family again. He had only found solace when he met and fell in love with Josh's mother. They shared their similar stories and were able to give comfort and understanding to each other.

When they married, they pledged to have as many children as possible to rebuild the tribe, which had been brutally obliterated. One of four children, Josh knew that his parents wanted an even larger family, but his mother had been advised that to continue could endanger her health.

The Hart's four grandsons were chatting amongst themselves, but Haylee was paying close attention to their conversation. 'What is Kindertransport?' she asked Josh.' I know what kinder egg is.'

'Unfortunately it is something very different.' Josh looked at Hal inquiringly, as if to ask if he should continue. Hal nodded imperceptibly. Josh tried to choose his words carefully; in order to make a horrendous situation more palatable to an eleven year old's ears.

'The word *kinder* means child in German. Conditions were becoming increasingly harsh and unpleasant for Jews in Germany and Austria, just before the Second World War broke out. Lots of parents decided that hard as it was, they would send their children abroad to safety. This became known as the Kindertransport.

Up to the day war broke out, about ten thousand Jewish children were put on trains for the long, frightening journey to England. On arrival, they were sent to foster homes, farms and hostels. My father at age seventeen was one of the oldest to come and was totally alone.'

'Why only children,' Haylee asked?

'That was the rule of the British government. They offered shelter to those who would not be a burden on the state, and children under the age of seventeen fell into that category.'

'Those poor children, how frightening for them' Haylee commented then added with remarkable perception 'and how terrible for their parents. It must have been very difficult to say goodbye to their children, not knowing when and if they would see them again. I know how my mum cried just waving goodbye to us for a week's cruise. How did the children manage once they arrived in England?'

'Well, from ten thousand children there were ten thousand different stories. Historians have tried to record as many as possible. My mother was also on the Kindertransport and was just 16 when she went over with her younger sister. They were sent to a large castle with three hundred other children, where they were all well-looked after. Sadly, not everyone had a good experience.'

Many of the heart-breaking stories he had heard from his parents came crowding back into his mind. Josh recalled them talking about how the kindertransport children tried to find out the fate of their parents after the war. A few lucky ones were reunited, but the majority, his own parents included, had to face the devastating realization that the loved ones left behind had all perished.

With the arrival of their food there was a lull in the conversation and they all tucked in hungrily. Hal spoke again as he told Josh wistfully that his singing had been so uplifting, bringing back many memories from his childhood.

'Do you know the origins of that tune for Lechu Dodi?'

'Yes. It's unique and hauntingly beautiful,' Josh replied. 'There is a poignant story behind it. The music was written by Avraham Kohn, cantor of the Klaus Shul in Mannheim, who included it in the Synagogue choir's songbook. On Kristallnacht the Shul was set alight and everything went up in flames. Miraculously, the book was salvaged by two brothers, Shlomo and Yosef Stein. They were not able to return it to Avraham at that time, because he was arrested that night, together with all his family. Fortunately they were all released and managed to leave Germany. The Stein brothers made their way to Israel, bringing the songbook with them, and after many years of searching, located members of the Kohn family and returned the book to them.'

Grandpa Hal, clearly moved by the story, excused himself for a few minutes, saying he was feeling a little overcome by the heat.

'I'll just go outside to cool off.'

As soon as he left, Haylee turned to Josh and Alistair.

'Will you come to Grandpa's surprise 70th birthday party next month?'

'I'd love to,' Josh replied, 'but I'll be back in England. Funnily enough, my 70th birthday is also next month, on Christmas Day to be precise.' The children all exclaimed together, 'that's grandpa's birthday as well.' At that point Hal returned. Amidst exuberant chatter they informed him that Joshy Boy's 70th birthday was on the same day as his. At the end of the evening, Hal and Esther told Josh that they were looking forward to seeing him in Shul again for morning prayers.

Back in the cabin, out of curiosity Josh took another look at the itinerary which included details of Esther's art class. He imagined that behind the modest and unassuming exterior as an art teacher and grandma, there was a deeply thoughtful and talented lady.

"*We are greatly privileged to have with us many distinguished passengers, including Esther Hart R.A. a renowned artist, who has volunteered to give a light-hearted class entitled "Art for Beginners." Esther is an intrepid and adventurous artist having travelled to many fascinating locations in order to document layers of history. Her observational scenes tell the stories of the places she has visited and the people she has met, all painted with remarkable insight. Her work has been exhibited in numerous countries and has garnered praise at the highest echelons of artistic critique.*

Chapter Twenty Seven

"The Sea is only the embodiment of a supernatural and wonderful existence."
Jules Verne

Saturday 23rd November 2019. At Sea

Josh exceeded even his own expectations with his rendition of the weekly Torah reading. He was gratified by the accolades from all present at the end of the service. At home, in his own shul his efforts were simply taken for granted. He had forgotten how good it felt to be appreciated and complimented. He noticed with disappointment that Hal was missing, knowing how much he had been looking forward to being there.

'Hal didn't feel well and stayed in bed', Esther informed him, 'but the grandchildren are taking good care of him.'

Out of a vast choice of activities, Josh decided to spend the final day at sea taking a tour called "*Heartbeat of the Operation*," which offered a glimpse behind the scenes of the huge ship. The catering manager met the group in the foyer of deck three. He promised to take them through the choreography involved in keeping more than four thousand guests fed, housed and content, whilst floating in the middle of the sea for a week. Leading them down long corridors, which he called the secret highway, they accompanied him until reaching the kitchens and storerooms.

'When the ship returns to its home port after seven days at sea, reloading new supplies, with a budget of over a million dollars can take about eight hours. Our chefs often go down to the docks to taste the wares randomly, to ensure that everything is of the finest quality. A combination of art and science guarantees that we fulfil every need of our passengers, whilst at the same time minimizing waste. Would you like some statistics?'

Without waiting for their response he reeled off a list of the staggering quantities required for twenty thousand meals prepared every day.

'During a week-long cruise we can go through two hundred and fifty thousand eggs, ten thousand pounds of chicken, fifteen thousand pounds of beef and one hundred and seventy thousand pounds of fresh fruit. The list is endless. As you can see, stocks are running low as we come to the end of the cruise. Fresh bread is baked on board every day and we have a famous chocolatier who produces exclusive creations each day.'

At the end of the tour, returning to his room Josh bumped into Haylee, who was on her way to visit her grandfather.

'Mind if I join you for a few minutes?' Josh asked.

'Oh yes please. Do come, he will be so happy to see you. He hasn't stopped talking about you.' A few minutes extended to more than an hour. Hal and Josh talked, joked and when Josh noticed Hal's pain and discomfort, he sang to him. Josh finally took his leave with fond farewells.

Remembering that Alistair had mentioned something about registering for a talent contest, Josh returned to his cabin to consult the daily communique and took himself to the relevant venue. The show was just beginning. All sorts of hopefuls were entertaining the audience, singing, dancing, juggling and joking, but Alistair was the undisputed star. He cleverly combined humorous anecdotes with comedic celebrity impersonations. The finale to his routine, in typical Alistair fashion, was somewhat audacious. His face covered in orange makeup, hair combed into a high quiff, he bellowed in Trump's unmistakable voice 'Melania, how many times do I need to tell you not to use my makeup!'

Chapter Twenty Eight

"Determine that the thing can and shall be done,
and then we shall find the way"
Abraham Lincoln

Sunday 24th November 2019. Fort Lauderdale

At the end of the cruise the ship docked at Fort Lauderdale. During disembarkation, Josh and Alistair noticed Damien standing on the dock with the purser and two policemen. They went over to see if they could help. The police were questioning him over the whereabouts of his wife Dee, who evidently was not disembarking with him. Damien explained that she had stayed in Jamaica, however the purser pointed out that Dee had not reclaimed her passport. He further emphasized that scrupulous records were kept and no one could leave or board the ship without it being registered. There was no record of her leaving the ship in Jamaica.

Damien stated resolutely that she was alive and well, staying with her friend and provided the police with her contact details in Jamaica. At that point Josh and Alistair left, confident that the issue would be speedily resolved. It was then that they noticed an ambulance parked on the dock with five familiar pirates standing nearby. As they approached, Haylee ran up to tell them that Grandpa Hal was not well and was being taken to hospital. They asked Esther if there was anything they could do. She thanked them, but was sure that their two sons would meet them at the Fort Lauderdale Hospital.

With a whole day to spend in Fort Lauderdale before their night flight to Tel Aviv, they decided to take a Hop-on Hop-off bus tour round the city, having deposited their luggage at the cruise terminal for the day. Towards the end of the tour, they passed the Fort Lauderdale Hospital. Spontaneously they decided to visit Hal and see how he was doing.

They were greeted with a cheery smile from a friendly lady at reception with the name 'Jenny' emblazoned on her tag. She located the name on her computer and informed them that Hal had been transferred to the oncology department. With explicit directions they set off. Making countless left and right turns, crossing innumerable internal bridges and going up one lift then down in another, they were mortified some fifteen minutes later to find themselves back where they had started, facing Jenny. Greatly amused by their embarrassment she drew them a map to follow.

On their second attempt they found Hal's ward, but could see all the family outside in tears, attempting to console each other. Clearly they had been given bad news.

'I don't think we should intrude on their grief.' Alistair commented. Josh agreed but as they started to walk away, Esther saw them and called after them. Despite her tears she put her arm on Josh's sleeve, saying how grateful she was to him. Hal had been so calm and content after the Friday night service. Josh had reminded him of the melody he had not heard since his childhood, evoking many happy memories. He had gone to bed singing it over and over.

His condition had deteriorated through Saturday night, but they had laid awake, side-by-side as he talked about his grandfather, his bar-mitzvah and his family. Josh was extremely moved by her words and wondered if this was yet another sign.

As they started to move away a sad, tear-stained Haylee came over to them.

'Josh, do you have a granddaughter of my age?' He had to think for a minute.

'Yes Bracha Tova is eleven.'

'Would you mind if I write a short note to her?'

'Of course not' Josh replied, impressed by her unabashed self-confidence. They waited patiently while she removed a pen and paper from her backpack. In a few minutes she filled up the page.

On return to the cruise depot, they retrieved their luggage and took a taxi to Miami airport for their night flight to Tel Aviv.

Settled into their seats, Josh remembered Haylee's letter. It occurred to him that she might have made reference to "Joshy Boy" which could provoke some unwanted queries, so he decided to read it.

Dear Bracha Tova,
You don't know me but I met your grandfather on our cruise. I am feeling very sad because my gramps died today. He was very special and I will always miss him. He would have been seventy on December 25th this year and we were going to make him a surprise party. I know I am going to cry on that day instead of it being a celebration. Your grandpa told us he is seventy on the same day and I think he is very special too, so I hope you will be having a party, then I can think about that and not feel so sad.
Haylee
PS I would love to be your pen pal as I understand we are the same age. Would you like to write to me?

Little cartoon characters decorated the letter, which presumably she had learnt from her artistic grandmother.

Josh was deeply moved by Haylee's sweet and thoughtful words. He showed the letter to Alistair who could not stop blubbering as he quoted from his favourite source;

"*Few parents nowadays pay any regard to what their children say to them. The old fashioned respect for the young is fast dying out.*"

Josh presumed those words had been written well over one hundred years earlier. Preparing for another long haul, Josh encouraged Alistair to expand on his 'comedy career'.

'Well, there were lots of very bright, very funny people in Footlights during my time at Cambridge, including a number who went on to become household names like Fry and Laurie. Some of us teamed up as double acts. I joined with someone else called Alistair, so, a bit like "*The Two Ronnies*", we were known as "*The Two Alistairs*". Not that we achieved their fame,' he hastened to add. 'Our humour was satirical rather than slapstick and we did a lot of impersonations.

When we left Cambridge, we took our show on the road for a few years. The other Alistair was very keen for us to appear at the Edinburgh Festival, but after my humiliation in that city, I was reluctant to return. In the end I agreed, aware of just how vast the Festival had grown, so that a chance meeting with anyone from Bonnie's family was highly unlikely.

'I presume you didn't meet any of them?'

'Well, here is the irony of the story. Bonnie's sister Kylie was still living at home and attending Edinburgh University. Presumably she recognised my name, which brought her to our first show. Afterwards, she came backstage to see me and the three of us ended up spending a lot of time hanging out together.

It was the most amazing experience to be in Edinburgh, soaking up the eclectic atmosphere. The festooned streets were packed with crowds, suffused with the liveliness and euphoria of it all. On every street corner talented artists sang, danced and juggled. Every hopeful aspirant from all fields of entertainment probably went there, with the dream of being discovered. Have you ever been, Josh?'

'No, unfortunately it would not be considered appropriate in the Haredi community.'

'Anyway, after spending some time together as a threesome the inevitable happened. She and Alistair became an item. Alistair and I continued traveling around the country for a while performing our show, but he was pining for Kylie and one day announced that they were engaged. He asked me to be his best man, but understood when I declined, explaining that the memories were still too raw for me to attend the wedding.

They settled in Edinburgh and I pursued a single career for a time, but it wasn't the same, I missed the comradery we shared.

'Do you still keep in touch?'

'Yes, every year we exchanged Christmas cards. Then two years ago, Kylie wrote to tell me that Alistair had died. She wanted to thank me for being instrumental in bringing her true soul mate to her. Together with the letter, she included a photo which I had never seen before. Kylie was a talented photographer and had managed to capture a defining moment in our career, when we were presented with a prestigious Festival Comedy award.

I was greatly distressed to hear about Alistair, but the photo helped me to mourn his death, whilst rejoicing in nostalgic memories of those unforgettable years.

'What happened to Bonnie and Angus?'

'They both married, so at least I didn't scar them for life!'

'Did you ever meet them again?'

'Kylie and Alistair sent me an invitation to their Ruby Wedding Anniversary party and begged me to come. I thought it would be embarrassing to meet Bonnie and Angus again, but nevertheless decided to go. It just shows how perceptions have changed over the years.

Instead of it being the elephant in the room, Bonnie recounted the story and it was the cause of uproarious hilarity to the guests. As it turned out, that party was one of my most unforgettable experiences. By popular demand, we re-enacted some of our old sketches, then improvised a new one taking that fateful New Year's Eve episode as its theme. That certainly helped to expunge any feelings of guilt that still lingered in my mind.'

With that, they both settled down for a sleep, waking up as they heard the announcement to fasten safety belts in preparation for landing in Tel Aviv.

Chapter Twenty Nine

"Life is really simple but we insist on making it complicated."
Confucius

Monday 25th November 2019. Israel

At Ben Gurion airport they made their way to the Hertz desk to collect the rented car Josh had booked. While the clerk dealt with their documents, they looked on in amusement at the neighbouring desk, where a lady was laboriously emptying the complete contents of her backpack. Numerous items of an intimate nature were strewn unabashedly across the counter, as she delved deeper into the crevices of her voluminous bag. Eventually, with a triumphant yell of 'found it' she produced her driving license. Looking up, recognition hit them all at the same moment.

'Gee, you boys again. Now you definitely have to buy me ice cream. How long are you staying in Israel?' Rica inquired.

'Just a few days' Josh replied.

'Any plans to visit Eilat? I've plenty of room in my apartment if you would like to come and stay and you do owe me an ice cream. Tell you what, here's my card, just call if you fancy a drive down. Maybe I can even interest you in buying an apartment overlooking the sea. Once they give me a car, I'll be on my way. It only takes about four hours. I would prefer driving my own car but it was involved in an accident, so I took it in for major repairs before I went to China. I love the freedom of driving across the desert, imagining Moses leading the children of Israel, as they wandered for forty years.' She prattled on, undaunted that her audience was not totally attentive. 'Well, I'm off now. Look forward to seeing you in Eilat' she called out cheerily, taking her leave.

The receptionist at the Tel Aviv Hilton greeted Josh and Alistair warmly and promised that their valued possessions would be stored away safely. Settling into their bedrooms, Josh was taken aback by the sound of the internal phone ringing.

'Was there a reason you chose this hotel.'

'One of the best, why?'

'Nothing to do with the beach?' Alistair asked with amusement in his voice.

'No' Josh replied, slightly puzzled.

'Look out of your window at the flags flying down there.' Josh was indeed amused as he saw all the flags with red, green, blue, yellow, orange and violet stripes, fluttering in the wind. They were overlooking the gay beach.

Josh was pleased to offer his services as a tour guide to Alistair. Admittedly, his knowledge of Israel was in no way comparable to Alistair's profound understanding of China and its culture, but that would not deter him from sharing his love for the country.

They drove to Jerusalem, where Alistair was enthralled, as Josh pointed out the many holy sites Alistair had read about. Visiting Mea Shearim, a strictly orthodox area, Josh wanted to give him a glimpse into the sort of lifestyle Josh's family led. Wandering through the streets, Alistair expressed admiration at how well-behaved the children appeared to be.

Mothers and fathers were accompanied by numerous children, all walking in neat formation behind them. Josh explained that the apparently disciplined behaviour was thanks to their insular upbringing.

'They don't have televisions, so the children are not exposed to violence. From the cradle, they see their parents praying devoutly and learn how to do the same. The parents generally aren't prone to screaming at each other or at the children. All these factors help to create a calm environment and a calm child. To a large extent they are sheltered from mayhem and violence by living in their protective bubble. Most are content with Torah study and prayer as their life force. Sex is a taboo subject. Very often, a young bride and groom have only met once or twice before they marry. Rarely if ever, have they been in the same room with someone of the opposite sex, apart from siblings, and find it very difficult to be thrust into the intimacies of marriage. Gradually they learn to adapt and in the most part are totally at peace with their lives. The problem comes when a person wants to leave the fold. Then you have someone like me who has managed to embrace Haredi, modern orthodox and secular lifestyles. Modern Orthodox Judaism is open to outer society living a more realistic life, aware of what is going on.'

The rest of the day was spent pleasurably at the Israel Museum. Alistair had brought his book of snuff bottles with him, on the off chance that he might be able to show it to the curator. Not only did he manage to show the book to the museum hierarchy but it stirred up great interest. A suggestion that Alistair present an exhibition of his collection was greeted with delight.

Chapter Thirty

"Our greatest glory is not in never falling,
but in rising up every time we fall."
Nelson Mandela

Tuesday 26th November 2019. Yad Mordechai

'Now I remember!' Alistair exclaimed excitedly, 'now I remember!' Josh looked up expecting elaboration.

'I had a Jewish friend at Cambridge called Rebecca. We belonged to the same GO club and were great friends as well as great rivals.'

'What is GO?' Josh asked curiously.

'It's an abstract strategy board game, originally developed in China two thousand five hundred years ago. The board consists of black lines running horizontally and vertically and each player takes turns in placing stones of their own colour on the intersection of the lines, one stone at a time. Considering that it is one of the oldest board games still played, it's surprising how few people seem to have heard of it.

One year, we were chosen to represent England at the international GO championships in Japan. We spent a fascinating week exploring Tokyo together, in between matches. When Rebecca left Cambridge we occasionally kept in touch by letter, and the last I heard she had married an Israeli and went to live on his kibbutz. I've been trying to remember the name of the kibbutz and it has just come to me. It was Mordechai. I remember, because I always thought it was funny that her husband had the same name as the kibbutz.'

'Ah, it must be Yad Mordechai.'

'Yes that's it, but I don't suppose she will still be there.'

'There's a strong possibility that she would be. The kibbutz system offers incentives to the children of members encouraging them to stay, so she and even her children and grandchildren might still be living there. Give me her name and I'll call the office to see if she is still a member.'

Josh called the kibbutz office and asked if Rebecca Shani still lives there.

'That must be Rivka Shani, hold on and I'll transfer the call.' Josh handed the phone to Alistair telling him they were putting it through to Rivka Shani.

The moment he heard her voice he knew it was Rebecca. Despite supreme efforts at Cambridge to cultivate her accent, she could never totally disguise the dulcet tones of her Geordie heritage. 'ALISTAIR 'she cried in disbelief 'where are you?' Her joy was boundless when he told her he was in Israel.

'You must come here and I'll show you around. This is a very important Kibbutz in Israel's history. I know you will find it fascinating. I can't wait to see you, can you come today?' Since they had not made plans for the rest of the day, it seemed the ideal opportunity.

Rebecca, or Rivka as she was now known, was waiting impatiently at her front door as they arrived. Time swept away as the two old friends were caught up in the moment of their reunion. They spent a long time reminiscing about their times at Cambridge and their trip to Japan, whilst her family and members of the kibbutz popped in to greet her old friend. A running buffet of pita bread, salads, cheeses, eggs, fish and other assorted dishes was laid out for everyone to help themselves.

'Now it's time to take you round the kibbutz, it's actually quite sprawling.' She jumped on to a tractor parked outside her house and called Alistair and Josh to hop on.

Rivka apologized in advance for sounding too much like a tour guide, but amongst her other jobs on the kibbutz; she was also one of their official English guides.

'The kibbutz started in a different location, but moved to the present site in 1943 and was named in memory of Mordechai Anielewicz. He was the first commander of the Jewish Fighting Organization in the Warsaw Ghetto Uprising.'

As she spoke, she led them past the statue erected in his name. They continued on to the reconstructed site of the 1948 independence War battlefield. Leading them through the defence bunkers, they looked out over the battleground, displaying hundreds of stand-up cut-outs of soldiers with guns. Rivka commented proudly on the incredible bravery of the original kibbutz members during the 1948 War.

'The kibbutz was in a strategic position on a hill dominating the coastal road and consequently was the key target for the Egyptian troops advancing to Tel Aviv. Despite being merely 130 kibbutzniks, aided by only twenty Haganah fighters, they managed to repulse two thousand five hundred Egyptian soldiers who had the benefit of armour, artillery and air support.

After five exhausting days of shelling and attack, with many losses, the remaining kibbutz members withdrew from the kibbutz under cover of darkness. Not realising this, the next day the Egyptians resumed a four-hour artillery barrage on an empty kibbutz. Thanks to our brave kibbutzniks, they were successful in delaying the Egyptian advance, giving the newly-formed Israeli Defence Forces the time needed to push back the Egyptians and save Tel Aviv.'

As Rivka drove away from the area they passed cowsheds, chicken coups and orchards where citrus fruits were growing in abundance. She also pointed out houses built in an extension of the kibbutz, intended specially for the next generation and their growing families. Their final visit was to the apiary, where they could observe the process and preparation of the honey for which Yad Mordechai was famous throughout the land. Arriving back at Rivka's house she asked Alistair if he still played GO?'

'No, I haven't played for years, how about you?' 'Nor me, but I still have a board. How about a game for old time's sake?' They set up the board on the table at the front of the house, and word quickly spread round the kibbutz that Rivka was playing GO against her old Cambridge friend. None of the members on the kibbutz had ever heard of the game, but that didn't deter them from coming to cheer Rivka on. She was a brilliant mathematician, a great advantage when playing GO and Alistair had only managed to beat her on rare occasions. It would be a matter of pride to him if he could vanquish his nemesis.

As the game progressed, Alistair perceived that he might be beating her, but looking up at her friends all willing her to win, he knew that it would be a Pyrrhic victory to crush her in front of them. The cheers which erupted when she was declared the winner confirmed his instincts. As a consolation offering, she gave them each a jar of honey, imploring them to come back soon.

Chapter Thirty One

"Life is either a daring adventure or nothing at all."
Helen Keller

Wednesday 27th November 2019. Rishon Lezion

Picking up a newspaper at breakfast, Josh commented that he had hardly read one since leaving home. Turning over the page, a headline took his breath away. "Philanthropist Damien Montague arrested on suspicion of murder" He read the article to Alistair.

> *'Evidence is mounting up against diamond magnate Damien Montague on suspicion of murdering his wife Dee by throwing her overboard on a Caribbean cruise. Fort Lauderdale security officers were alerted when Dee didn't reclaim her passport and Damien left the cruise ship alone. He asserted that his wife had decided to stay with a friend in Jamaica. On verification, the contact details he gave for the friend did not exist and there was no record of his wife leaving the ship there. Passengers have been contacted by email to ask for any information they might have regarding her whereabouts.'*

Josh read on.

'A photo of the couple had been included with the email. As a result one passenger had come forward, stating that he had occupied the adjoining cabin and had heard sounds of fierce arguments. Further damning evidence came from a couple whom Damien and Dee had befriended at dinner the night before they docked in Jamaica. The couple told the police that they had accompanied Dee and Damien to a bar for cocktails, but just as they ordered their drinks, Dee felt dizzy and needed to feel the cool sea air on her face. She asked Damien to take her outside, but he returned ten minutes later alone, dishevelled and with a fresh scratch mark on his face. He explained that Dee had fallen over and returned to their cabin. According to Damien, she had tripped near the railings, almost pulling him down with her, badly cutting her knee, as well as scraping his face accidentally with her diamond ring. 'My fault,' he had joked, 'for giving her the finest rock from my collection.'

Helpfully, the couple were able to pinpoint the door near to the bar where Dee and Damien had exited. The cameras were carefully scrutinized, clearly showing Dee and Damien walking towards the ship's railings and their ensuing scuffle. In a clip eight minutes later Damien could be seen alone.'

Alistair was plainly becoming more and more agitated and concerned about the news report.

'Josh I think I might have some important evidence which could help Damien. I was in the reception lobby the day before we docked in Jamaica. I saw Dee working on a computer and writing on a piece of paper. I went over to say hello, but she seemed distracted and dropped her notes. I picked them up for her and saw they were in Chinese. Now I hadn't mentioned to her that I understand Chinese, because she comes from Macau, where they speak Cantonese, not Mandarin, although the written language is the same. Obviously she had no reason to hide her notes from me and I noticed that it was a list of flights leaving Jamaica, complete with times and dates commencing from the day we were docking. I also noticed an address in Macau, Rua de S Miguel 65, which was actually written in English. This stuck in my mind because I've a friend called Miguel aged 65. I have to contact the police in Fort Lauderdale to tell them. After all, if the waiter in Belize had not given evidence on my behalf, I could still be languishing in jail.'

'I suggest you call them a little later today, it's still the middle of the night there. In the meantime, I hope you will join me on my sentimental journey to Rishon, the place where I spent five magical years.'

In Rishon, driving down the tree-lined street with overhead branches from both sides entwining in the middle,

Josh reminisced on his happiness every time he had returned from a weekend in London. As he neared the block of flats, he thought about their next door neighbour Dora Strauss, a sprightly octogenarian who had survived the Holocaust. Although she never spoke of her past, the six-numbered blue tattoo engraved on her arm spoke volumes. He remembered Dora's eightieth birthday party. He and Yang had racked their brains to try and come up with an original gift. All of their ideas paled into insignificance when her daughters announced that they had booked a paragliding ride for their indomitable mum. When Dora returned, the fearless eighty year-old had told Josh that it had been one of the most exciting and exhilarating days of her life. She must be long gone by now, he sighed to himself.

Outside his former flat and emerging from the car, he was totally confused as he looked longingly up at the first floor. The building he had lived in was now replaced by a stylish pebble-dashed block, complete with balconies. His mind went back to the contentment he had felt, sitting by the front window, smoking his pipe and watching the world go by.

He heard his name being called and looked round. Shielding his face from the bright November sun, he looked up. Surely it could only be an apparition, but no, there was Dora Strauss standing on her balcony, exuberantly waving a walking stick and calling his name. He indicated his pleasure at seeing her again as she shouted down to him.

'You simply must come up for coffee' to which he replied that he had a friend waiting for him in the car.

'Bring him up; I can't let you go without seeing you.' Calling to Alistair to join him, they entered the front door, where his confusion intensified. He had assumed that the old block had been demolished and replaced by a new one, but the interior had an old familiarity to it. He climbed the same staircase, although refurbished, that he had climbed so many times before, but instead of going to the right-hand flat, this time he went to the one on the left. The door was opened by a sweet-faced girl with Philippine features, and Dora waved them over to join her on the balcony. After warm greetings Josh asked Dora about the changes in the property.

'Haven't you heard of Tama 38?' she asked in her flawless English. 'It is a project designed to strengthen old buildings against earthquakes and at the same time giving the whole facade a face lift. A contractor takes on the project and in return is permitted to add one or two extra floors, which he sells at a profit. So it's a win-win situation.'

'What an ingenious scheme' Josh said as he looked around in admiration at the modern flat which now replaced her previously tired and slightly shabby home.

'Did you move out during the renovations?'

`We were encouraged to and offered incentives. Most of the neighbours did, but you know me, I am a stubborn old mule so I stayed. I must admit though, it was a nightmare and for eighteen months it was like living in a bomb site. Corrugated iron sheets lined the stairwell, the lift shaft was an open space and exposed electricity wires were everywhere. Those were a few of the inconveniences I suffered, but I've lived through worse,' she added plaintively. 'I went out as little as possible and I have my guardian angel here all the way from the Philippines to help me.' At that point she called out 'Joumana'

'Yes Mammy' came the endearing response.

'Please make our guests a drink and let them taste your delicious baking.'

Graciously pouring tea from a teapot, Dora was undoubtedly thrilled to see Josh again. Inquisitive to hear about his life and his lovely girlfriend, she hardly gave Josh time to answer all her questions before she continued.

'It always gave me great comfort at night, knowing you were there next door. I could hear the muffled sounds of your voices through our adjoining wall. Not that I was listening,' she added with a twinkle in her eye, 'but I felt safer when you were there. I always felt lonely at the end of the week when you both went away.'

Josh had been listening with half an ear as his mind went on one of its detours but he picked up on her last words.

'Both went away,' he repeated in shock.

'Yes' she went on, oblivious to his reaction. 'I would hear you going off late on Thursday evening to catch your night flight, and hear a taxi bringing you back in the early hours of Monday morning. Then, on Friday, I would see Yang leave with her overnight bag, and look forward to the reassuring sounds of her return, every Saturday night.' Josh was totally dumbfounded by Dora's words. Yang had always told him that she spent lonely hours in their flat waiting for him to come back.

Shortly afterwards they took their leave with Josh's mind in a whirl. Could she have been unfaithful to him? He knew it was ludicrous to still care, but he simply had to discover the truth. The thought that Yang might have had another lover was excruciating to him. The only way he could think of to discover the truth, short of asking Yang herself, was to ask Sammy.

Driving away, Josh managed to quell his turbulent thoughts. Alistair had given him some fascinating insights into China and its history and now he wanted to reciprocate in Israel.

'First of all, we are going to visit a unique ecological project. For years this was one of Israel's biggest eyesores, a polluted dumping mound for the nation's garbage, visible for miles around, but now you will see how it has been transformed.'

The Ariel Sharon Park, viewed from a slightly elevated vantage point, was indeed impressive. It had been turned into a picturesque park with a lake, picnic areas, hiking and bicycle trails, shady groves and a colourful display of flowers and plants. There was simply no comparison to its previous image, captured in the photographs on display.

Leaving the park, Josh commented 'Since you found the history of Yad Mordechai so fascinating, we're going to visit another insightful part of Israel's early history. An entire underground munitions factory was constructed and hidden under a kibbutz laundry. The bullets manufactured there were used in order to achieve Israel's independence. Alistair was intrigued, prompting Josh to call The Ayalon Institute in advance, to book a guided tour.

The tour started in the laundry room where they were shown how a washing machine was moved aside, revealing a concealed spiral staircase leading down to an enormous area. Here, kibbutz members had worked ceaselessly day and night making bullets. The guide revealed that more than four million had been produced during the three years of manufacturing. The whole space was filled with life-like figures and artefacts from bygone days, including machines which groaned into action as the visitors were given a demonstration. The precarious position of the kibbutz next to a British army base had initiated all kinds of subterfuge, to mislead the British soldiers, who often came to visit the pretty young girls on the kibbutz.

Chapter Thirty Two

"True compassion is more than flinging a coin to a beggar; it comes to see that an edifice which produces beggars needs reconstructing."
Martin Luther King Jr.

Thursday to Saturday 28th to 30th November 2019. Eilat

'How about we complete our epic journey with a trip to Eilat?'

Josh was not totally surprised when Alistair made this suggestion, or hare-brained scheme as Josh had now come to regard some of Alistair's ideas.

'Despite her quirks and eccentricity, Rica is good company and I bet she would make a gracious hostess.'

'I suppose we could drive down today,' Josh suggested dubiously, 'coming back after Shabbat or early Sunday morning in good time for the concert. My only concern is the sort of food she might serve. I can imagine her presenting us with shellfish for Friday night supper.'

'Let me speak to her,' Alistair suggested, 'I can occasionally be tactful!'

'Okay,' Josh responded, still slightly sceptical about the whole proposition. 'Just one thing though, I am NOT sharing a double bed with you, so please tell her that you were joking about our loving liaison!'

After a long conversation, Alistair declared 'All arranged. When I said we were coming down and staying in a hotel, she wouldn't hear of it. I told her why it might be awkward for you and she assured me that she keeps kosher. She often entertains religious friends for Friday night supper. I also revealed the true nature of our collaboration!'

'Did she sound upset that we had misled her?'

'On the contrary, she sounded delighted. I've a suspicion that she might have designs on one of us for spouse number four!'

'But you did tell her that I am married and you are gay?'

The sheepish look on Alistair's face gave Josh the answer.

'Anyway a leopard can change his spots.'

I rather think the expression is that a leopard CAN'T change its spots,' Josh pointed out.

'Well perhaps this one can! I know of many gay people who marry. Even Oscar married and had children.'

'Alistair, you know I hold you in the highest esteem, but why on earth would Rica be interested in a non-Jewish, gay, geriatric who lives in Rome with his dog, parrots, antiquities and housekeepers?'

'With all due respects Josh, why did a 25 year-old, non-Jewish Chinese girl fall for an aging Haredi man, married with a multitude of progeny?'

'Touché! Point taken, but please tell me you are only joking about Rica.'

Is it such a ridiculous idea?' I could even convert. Do you still have your mohel equipment?'

'Now I know you are joking. Ok I will go and pack. I just want to send an email to Sammy first. I know it seems irrelevant now, but I must know where Yang went to every Shabbat.

They broke the long drive to Eilat at Mitzpe Ramon, where Josh wanted to show Alistair the Makhtesh Ramon Visitor Centre. Built on a small hill overlooking the Ramon crater, it was dedicated to Israel's famous astronaut Ilan Ramon, who had sadly died in the 2003 Columbia Space Shuttle disaster. Ilan Ramon's name was originally Wolferman but because of his deep love of the area, he changed it to Ramon.

The exhibition highlighted Ilan's many accomplishments and was also in memory of his son Asaf Ramon. Six years after the space shuttle tragedy had claimed his father's life, the F16 jet that Asaf was piloting crashed, not very far from Mitzpeh Ramon.

The rest of the journey through the stark backdrop of the Negev was uneventful. They located Rica's luxurious penthouse without a problem thanks to Waze. Despite her idiosyncrasies, Rica was indeed a warm and welcoming hostess greeting them with exuberance.

Allaying Josh's initial reservations, Rica served a sumptuous, strictly kosher, Friday night dinner. An array of tasty dishes was stylishly proffered on unusual platters, which she had collected on her travels. Her other guests were a diverse gathering of friends who clearly held her in high esteem and were keen to hear about her holiday exploits.

After China, Rica told them she had flown to India where she met a cousin, who until recently she hadn't even known existed. She told them how she had made contact by sending away for a DNA kit from a genealogical site. After sending back the test they informed her of various hits, including a first cousin. Josh made a mental note of the name of the website, wondering if by an unlikely chance, he could have any unknown relatives out there.

When they returned from Eilat Alistair found messages from both the FBI and an exceptionally grateful Damien.

With the evidence Alistair had given over the phone, the FBI intensified their investigation and dispatched police to the address in Macau. Indeed, Dee was found alive and well, living with her boyfriend Carlos. He claimed that he was also a victim of her elaborately-devised plan and was willing to give evidence against his erstwhile girlfriend, in return for clemency.

Macau, often referred to as the Las Vegas of Asia was home to many luxury hotels, each vying to be more extravagant than the others, with their themed attractions and luxury casinos. According to Carlos, Dee had a serious gambling habit and needed to fund her lavish lifestyle. His job as a croupier in the casino of the MGM Cotai Hotel made him an ideal accomplice in her meticulous plan. She had persuaded him to pinpoint rich, older men playing the tables. Despite living in the poor area of the city, Dee would emulate the wealthy clientele who were staying in the hotel, masquerading as a wealthy guest there. With help from Carlos, she found Damien, a diamond merchant. With disposable assets in the form of diamonds and no incumbent wives or children to thwart her intricately-woven scam, he suited her scheme perfectly.

Totally unsuspecting, Damien was enchanted by her charms and readily succumbed to her beauty. She told him she was a virgin and intended to save herself for marriage. It didn't take long before Damien had proposed and they were married soon after.

After the wedding the couple returned to South Africa. Having had no formal honeymoon Dee suggested booking a cruise, planning to remove all the diamonds from the safe just before their departure. Once on-board ship, her plan was to create a scenario which would lead to his arrest for her murder.

Artfully she had worked out each detail. Before leaving, she had persuaded Carlos to make a recording of fierce but indistinct arguments between a husband and wife. She would wait until Damien was happily ensconced in the casino, before playing the recording in the hope that it would be heard by anyone passing by, or in the neighbouring cabins.

In order to leave the ship in Jamaica undetected, more devious plans had been implemented involving disguise, subterfuge, bribery and deception. For the most condemning part of the plan, she had chosen a friendly couple to invite to a bar for a drink in the anticipation that they would give testimony later.

Leading an innocent, trusting Damien to the ship's railings, she feigned dizziness, stumbling against him, making it look like a scuffle. As she grabbed his arm and ruffled his clothes she scratched his face with her ring. Telling him that she would go back to the cabin to lie down, he must return to the bar and explain the mishap to the couple. She had chosen the position by the railings carefully, to ensure that the security camera would pick up their scuffle, knowing that she would not be caught on camera when she went off in the other direction.

Had it not been for Alistair, her ruse could well have succeeded and poor Damien might still be in prison protesting his innocence.

Chapter Thirty Three

"The only thing worse than being blind
Is having sight but no vision."
Helen Keller

Sunday 1st December 2019. Tel Aviv

Plagued by tortured thoughts throughout the night, Josh shared his anxieties with Alistair the next morning.

'Just like Damien was allured by Dee's seductive femininity, was I duped by Yang? Did she simply use me for free board and lodgings during the week, going off to be with her lover once I was safely out of the way?' Josh was becoming more and more convinced. 'I certainly wouldn't be the first man to be led astray by a temptress. Wasn't Eve responsible for the fall of man, representing desire and shame?'

Feeling quite despondent he went off to open his emails, reading the first one with stunned disbelief.

"My name is Lawrence. Sammy asked me to reply on his behalf, because his English is not good enough to answer legibly:"

"Yang travelled to Bnei Brak every Friday before the Sabbath to stay with a strictly-orthodox family, with the intention of converting to Judaism. She didn't want to tell you because she thought you would be upset and try to

discourage her. Despite you telling her many times that you would never leave your family, she still harboured the hope that you might reconsider, if she converted to Judaism. In the end, she sadly accepted that you could never do so."

Josh was flooded with a mixture of emotions, enormous guilt at his suspicions, yet great solace, knowing that far from being unfaithful, Yang had genuinely loved him. He compared their relationship to that of Damien and Dee and knew how lucky he had been. Despite their startling similarities in appearance, Yang could not have been more dissimilar from the devious, scheming Dee.

With obvious pleasure, Josh greeted his old friend outside the concert hall and introduced him to Alistair, before finding their seats in the spacious auditorium. The orchestra played a couple of introductory pieces before the conductor welcomed Yakira to the stage amidst deafening applause. She looked breath-taking in a silver gown, elegantly simple while accentuating the contours of her body. Josh was mesmerized.

Seating herself at the grand piano, she played a number of pieces, before surprising the audience by addressing them in fluent Hebrew. She explained that she had learnt the language when she lived in Israel for a number of years. She went on to say that this was a very special evening. Her daughter Jojo aged nine and a half was making her debut as a soloist playing Beethoven's Violin Sonata Number Nine, at which Yakira would accompany her on the piano. She had promised Jojo that their first stage appearance together would be in Israel, because this is where Jojo had been conceived. Even though they could no longer be together, she still loved Jojo's father very much. She had chosen the stage name Yakira because it meant precious in Hebrew and it reminded her of the precious years she had spent here with him.

Uncontrollable tears streamed down Josh's face as he grasped the fact that it was his daughter on the stage, wowing the audience with her virtuosity and musical abilities.

Remembering how ecstatic Yang had been when she thought she was pregnant, the truth hit him and it suddenly all made sense. To his surprise at the time, she had made an appointment with the gynaecologist, telling Josh it was just for a check-up. She had obviously asked him to remove the contraceptive device. The secret Sammy was holding back from him wasn't something sinister, or the existence of a husband. It was a daughter.

Amidst endless applause the concert was almost over, but the audience wanted more and more. Yang came back for the final explosive climax of her performance, transporting Josh to a musical paradise. He knew that she couldn't possibly be aware of his presence, but he sensed that her rapturous and sensual emotions were speaking directly to him through her music. Josh's mind was in turmoil. Not only had he found her, but the words she had spoken reflected a deep and abiding love for him. When he had embarked on this reckless journey, despite all his daydreams, he had never actually prepared himself for this eventuality.

Now he was faced with a tumultuous, painful decision. Did he have the emotional strength to make the sensible choice, the logical conclusion? Walk away and return to his wife and family. Yet an impetuous torrent of desire was running through his veins, telling him to listen to his heart. It wasn't too late in life to grab a vestige of happiness. Why not live out the rest of his days enveloped in a cocoon of love and devotion. He knew that once he revealed himself to Yang and their daughter he would never want to walk away from them. It was foolhardy, but the mantra which had propelled him on this journey was back again. Indeed, when, if not now?

Epilogue

"There are men and women who make the world better just by being the kind of people they are. They have the gift of kindness
or courage or loyalty or integrity. It really matters very little whether they are behind the wheel of a truck or running a business or bringing up a family.
They teach the truth by living it."
James A. Garfield

Love or Duty? Josh knew deep down that he must sacrifice his own personal longings. He had a moral duty to his family and could not put his own gratification first. Once home, he reverted to the life expected of him. All his grandchildren came to visit, to receive their gifts and were fascinated to hear about his travels through China and Belize. He faced a bombardment of questions. They were particularly interested to know how he had managed to observe all their religious strictures. Had he managed to pray at the appropriate times of day? How did he manage to find kosher food on his travels? Where had he spent each Shabbat? At least on that point he was able to elaborate truthfully, telling them about his fascinating meals with the Chabad family and his cousin.

Secreted in the privacy of his office, gazing at the painting which served as a nostalgic memento, he had time to reflect on his journey. Finally he could acknowledge to himself that he had actually managed to extinguish his yearnings and simply be happy with his lot.

He sent away for the DNA kit which he submitted, then waited patiently to see if there were any results.

Out of interest he decided to look up Alistair's name on the internet. He was still curious over Alistair's reticence to discuss how he knew the BBC interviewer, who they had met at the marriage market in Zhongshan Park. Could it be that Alistair had some dark, deep secret he wished to hide? Assuming that his name would be found in connection with his snuff bottle exhibition, to Josh's astonishment there was so much more about him. Josh prided himself as a master of deception by omission, but there was one aspect of Alistair's life that he had never mentioned.

"Sir Alistair Sylvester, heir to the family oil business, has been knighted by the Queen for his humanitarian efforts to society. He has financed the opening and ongoing maintenance of numerous safe havens for the poor and homeless all over Britain. These homes not only give shelter and health care to the residents, but also provide all basic needs to help break their daily cyclical battle to stay alive. A total and lengthy rehabilitation process, essential in order to restore their self-esteem, gave them the tools to become active members of society. When interviewed by the BBC, Sir Alistair said he was deeply honoured and humbled to be recognized in the Queen's list. 'I have been fortunate to meet so many dedicated and talented people.

Spending time helping others has given me the greatest fulfilment.'

He told the reporter that he knew how lucky he had been to be born into a privileged family, but homelessness could happen to anyone, if circumstances in their lives turned against them. In order to help them, he knew he had to see life from their perspective and he had spent many months living with these people who had lost all dignity.

'You cannot judge another person until you have been in his place. Only by sharing their tribulations was I able to fully appreciate their wretchedness.'

The article contained many details of his philanthropy in the UK over the years, despite him having relocated to Rome. A photo of his Italian villa was shown, nestling in acres and acres of verdant foliage in the foothills of Rome. There was even a rumour that he had built a complex of air-conditioned corridors throughout his garden, in order to exercise his dog when the weather was too hot and humid for him to be outside.

Josh read on. His two housekeepers are themselves testimony to the success of Alistair's philanthropy. They had been two lost and dispossessed souls who found each other during rehabilitation, fallen in love and decided to marry. On hearing their story, Alistair wanted to make a big celebration, in order to encourage others with the hope that a better life could be theirs. A spectacular wedding was organized, with all the residents of the home in attendance. Alistair had even arranged for his friend, who just happened to be a world-famous opera singer, to be flown from Italy to serenade the awestruck couple, as they walked down the aisle.

The more he read, it occurred to Josh that when Alistair had intimated he would like to help those street children in Belize, he already had an idea formulating in his mind.

January 2020

Dear Alistair or should I call you Sir Alistair? You are a dark horse!!!

Not only did you help me solve the mystery of Yang's disappearance, not only did you help me discover a daughter I never knew I had, but if it hadn't been for you I would never have located a whole branch of my mother's family whom we always thought had perished in the Holocaust.

Thanks to hearing Rica's story during our trip to Eilat, I was inspired to take a DNA test. This revealed that my mother had a brother who survived and the best part is that ....at 98 Uncle Ernie is still alive. Utilizing Zoom, Joshua and I have had an incredible face to face conversation with him. He told us how he went into hiding after Kristallnacht, not daring to go home, terrified that the Nazis were looking for him. He made his way to France, and after the fall of France, he joined the French Resistance and spent the rest of the war in rural areas of the forest. After the war he returned to our home town, only to be told that all the family had been wiped out in the Holocaust. He had no idea that two of his sisters had been sent to England. Likewise, they had no idea that he had survived. Subsequently he went to Australia, married and had six children, so we have discovered lots of cousins, AND how about this for a coincidence - one of his daughters actually married a Londoner, lives not far from us and our grandchildren even know each other!

There's more.......We told Uncle Ernie the story of the silver parrot spice container and I showed it to him. You just wouldn't believe how emotional he was when he saw it (well knowing you, you would!) as it evoked one of his favourite memories of my mother. He told us that at the end of every Shabbat my mother would fetch the beloved parrot for Havdalah and say "Off with his head" as she removed the head with great relish. After the ceremony she would always repeat: "All good things must come to an end and Shabbat is no exception. But don't worry; it will be back next week." Taken aback, Joshua told us that until her dying day, his mum said those words at the end of every Shabbat.

Uncle Ernie has sent me his memoirs in which he documents his early home life as well as events after that fateful night on November 9th 1938.

In my wildest dreams (and as you know there are many), I could never have visualised, thanks to our serendipitous encounter in Shanghai, where my journey would lead me. I can't tell you how much I value our friendship and appreciate the encouragement (and gentle cajoling!) you gave me every step of the way on our incredible travels.

Josh was elated when he received a reply from Alistair together with a photo of two similar snuff bottles side-by-side. Alistair elucidated that he had received a parcel containing the missing snuff bottle from the museum where they had been exhibited. It was accompanied by a letter of explanation. A hitherto-trusted member of their staff had been caught on camera stealing the snuff bottle and had relinquished it unharmed. The museum could not apologise sufficiently and trusted that he had not been put to too much inconvenience.

Alistair concluded with the news that he had just completed the house purchase in Belize.

Josh sent a short reply ending with the words

Did you see the news reported from Wuhan, China about the outbreak of a coronavirus disease? It looks like we left just in time!!

P.S. If you should ever need a British lawyer to dig you out of another hole……

Printed in Great Britain
by Amazon

70007735R00139